# Somewhe

Sassy, opinionated Shar Sinclair is passionate about the sea turtles she rescues in the Windswept Bay area and as needful of her freedom as they are. She's content with her life, helping run the family resort and looking out for the wildlife around her. But sometimes she wishes she had someone to share her passion, and passions with. But that might mean giving up some of her freedom and she's not sure she could do that for anyone...

Gage Lancaster is a self-made millionaire used to getting what he wants, but lately there's an emptiness and a restlessness to his life that he can't seem to fill. While visiting Windswept Bay, he spies a beautiful woman on the beach struggling to rescue a sea turtle tangled in fishing line and goes to help. Gage is captivated by the fire and passion that radiates from Shar and he knows instantly he wants her. But this may be one time when what he wants might not be an option.

Sparks fly on the sunset beach and sparkling blue waters of the romantic Windswept Bay as Gage and Shar battle through their attraction. Gage is determined that this is one time he'll do whatever it takes to get what he wants. But can Shar open her heart to him? Can he convince Shar that love doesn't mean shackles…but a lifetime shared with the one you love?

# SOMEWHERE WITH YOU

Windswept Bay, Book Two

# DEBRA CLOPTON

*Somewhere With You*

Copyright © 2016 Debra Clopton Parks

# CHAPTER ONE

Gage Lancaster strode out onto the deck of his rental, a three-story glass-and-wood monstrosity that Kym, his assistant, had rented for him on the spur of the moment. It sat on a semi-secluded beach on the tip of the small island of Windswept Beach. It was the perfect place for him to disappear.

And he'd done just that; having arrived here two days ago, he'd done nothing but hole up inside the house with no phones on, no TV, no Internet. He hadn't even opened the blinds during the day. Other than sitting in the dark on the deck at night and listening to the surf, he had for all intents and purposes gone off the grid.

Now, he rubbed his grizzled jaw, breathed in the sea air and decided it was probably time to start venturing out at least a little. The misty morning shrouded the coastline, making it impossible to see all the way across the bay where the main hub of the island was. He'd go check that out today. Right now, he was going to take advantage of the secluded beach and go for a quick dip in the ocean before his shower.

Going back inside, he cut the tags off a new pair of swim trunks with a knife from the kitchen, put them on and then strode back onto the deck. He pulled his shirt off over his head and dropped it in a lounge chair as he passed by and then he jogged down the steps and across the beach to the water's edge. For a little while, he was free: no phones to answer, no deals to manage, no contracts to sign. At least for a few days, no one other than Kym knew where he was.

And for now that suited him just fine.

He jogged into the surf and dove over a shallow wave into the blue water. He'd have to go back to real life soon. But not yet.

Not now.

For now, he was here.

He surfaced down the beach and turned to survey the coastline from the water. The exclusive homes on this stretch of shore were built for privacy and weren't easily visible from the water. Something else that suited him. He started to swim toward shore when he spotted a woman jogging toward the beach. She had shoulder-length dark hair that caught in the wind as she jogged. She ran beside a large, slightly humped rock and then dropped to her knees and started doing something. Curious, Gage swam toward shore. His feet had just touched sand when he realized it was a sea turtle that she was on her knees beside. A huge one.

She was struggling frantically with something on the turtle. Gage jogged out of the water; the shallow waves lapped at his legs as he headed toward the woman.

The turtle was tangled in twine and rope and she was struggling to free it.

A jolt of empathy washed over him and he jogged

through the remaining waves toward her. "Hey," he called when he was close enough for her to hear him.

She lifted her head and slammed him with angry eyes full of passion and fire. Her gaze raked over him, taking in his dripping appearance. His pulse jolted as those eyes met his and he slowed his pace and then stopped near her.

"Can you believe they just toss this overboard?" she snapped, then went back to work, so preoccupied it felt as though she hadn't really noticed he was there.

"Can I help? He looks like he's in a bad way."

Her head shot back up and those eyes singed his skin with the fire flaming there. "Yes." She stared at him. "It's hurting him and I need a knife. Or something to cut it off," she said, anxiously. "Look at his poor front foot. It'll probably have to be amputated."

Gage cringed at the foot that was so wrapped in the line that it was damaged horribly. "I have a knife." He reached for the pocket of his shorts for the pocketknife he always carried, the one his dad had given him many years ago. Only, he'd changed into the swim trunks, so he didn't have his knife. "Hang on. I'll be right back with a knife."

"Thank you. Hurry."

Gage raced across the sand to the rental, and not worrying whether he was dripping water on the tile, he went inside for a knife. He was running back across the beach in moments but it felt like hours. She was still struggling fruitlessly to remove the tangled mess, stopping to look up and see him jogging the last few feet.

He knelt beside her.

"Thank you." She reached for the knife. "I'll do it." It was clear she was strung tight with her passion to free the turtle and he let her have the knife. She bent over the foot that had line cutting into its skin and looked like a disaster. Gently, she began cutting away the line.

"People don't know the damage they're doing and the sea lives they are destroying when they are neglectful with trash and old lines." Her voice shook with frustration.

He saw that her hands shook too. "Here, let me." He gently covered her hands with his, stopping her movements. Electric shockwaves tore through him as he held her hands; when she lifted her gaze to his, everything in him hummed with the electrical charge.

She breathed in a short, shuddering breath and she nodded. "Okay. Just be careful. Be gentle."

He smiled. "I will be," he assured her. When she relinquished the knife and pulled her hands from his, he started to cut.

Working together, they soon had the line from the turtle and she inspected his wounds. "He's in bad shape. Looks like infection has set in. Poor big Loggerhead. They're protected because they were dying out a few years ago. And look at this poor thing—it's suffering from people's carelessness."

He heard her phone beep and she paused to tug it from her pocket. She read the message. Relief washed over her. "The ambulance is almost here. I can't thank you enough." As if on cue, a siren could be heard in the distance.

"An ambulance for the turtle?"

"Yes. I called them the moment I saw him lying there in trouble. We'll take him to the turtle hospital and they'll give it the care it needs and hopefully it will survive."

An orange ambulance careened over the rise and onto the beach. It moved slowly toward them across the sand. On the side it said, Windswept Bay Sea Turtle Hospital. He'd never seen anything like it. Then again, he'd never spent much time near the beach. He'd been too busy being holed up inside glass-and-steel buildings, making money. Today had been one of the few times that he'd ever swam in the ocean.

But not anymore. Today, he'd helped rescue a sea turtle, a Loggerhead, with a beautiful woman. He pushed the smile away. *Too serious a moment to think about that.*

"Hang in there, buddy," she urged the patient as she patted its shell, which rose a good twenty inches from the ground.

The ambulance wheeled around in a wide circle and backed up toward them. Feeling way out of his element, Gage watched the woman guide the ambulance toward them and then signaled it to halt steps away from them. She acted as if she'd done this before.

Immediately, a man hopped from the driver's seat and jogged toward them. He wore tan shorts and a faded red T-shirt with the Windswept Bay Sea Turtle Hospital insignia on the front.

"Shar," he said, as if he was well acquainted with the turtle-rescuing beauty. "Wow, you must have been in the right spot at the right time. He looks bad."

"He is, Alex. His front flipper is a mess," she said without preamble.

Another guy had unloaded from the passenger's side. He came around and opened the back doors of the ambulance.

"Man, he's a big one. Probably at least two hundred pounds, maybe two thirty. Let's load him up and get him some attention. Good work, Shar."

"Thanks, John. Glad you and Alex got here fast." Shar looked over at Gage. "Can you help?"

"Yeah, sure. Just tell me what to do."

Lifting a two hundred plus pound sea turtle was a chore even with four of them. But working together, they moved him onto a lift that was attached to the back of the ambulance and then it raised the turtle up and into the ambulance.

When it was loaded up, he was startled when Shar climbed into the ambulance with the turtle. "Thanks for your help. You were great out there." She shot him a dazzling smile as she lifted her hand in good-bye and then pulled the doors shut.

John and Alex thanked him again and then Gage watched the ambulance drive slowly over the sand. He could see Shar through the window as she focused on the turtle. The ambulance moved up the embankment and then disappeared, sirens blaring.

Gage didn't move. He watched the spot where the ambulance disappeared over the rise and wondered who Shar was.

It hadn't exactly been the opportune moment to ask for her name and phone number...but if she was that closely known by the guys at the hospital, then he knew where to find her.

And he would find her. There was no way he was going to forget her.

# CHAPTER TWO

Shar Sinclair slammed her car door and hurried toward the resort. Her heart was still hurting for the sea turtle. The surgeon had to amputate a large portion of the front flipper and put the turtle on massive doses of antibiotics from all the infection that had set in. It was very lucky that it had made it to her beach. She hadn't jogged in several days and hadn't been out looking for turtle eggs because of a twisted ankle that was still giving her some trouble. But today she'd been determined to get some exercise and to see whether any mama turtles had crawled onto the beach during the night and laid their eggs. Finding the beached loggerhead had been unexpected but thank goodness she'd been there.

Thank goodness *he* had been there.

She'd been so desperate to free the turtle but had realized her work was futile without a knife. And then she'd looked up and like an answer to prayer, there he was, this gorgeous guy calling out to her as he jogged from the water. Her heart had lodged in her throat and her stomach had dropped to her toes.

He was riveting…his muscles gleamed as he raked his hand through his short brown hair and getting water out of his pale-blue, Paul-Newman-eyes…he was that gorgeous.

And he was asking whether he could help her.

*Heck yeah.* And he'd jumped right in and been wonderful. She'd have to find him. Thank him. She'd been so zeroed in on the turtle that she'd half ignored him, and left without getting his name. But she'd been grateful that he'd been there. Grateful that he'd had the lean muscle of a man who might have been able to lift the turtle by himself if he'd tried.

"Shar, you're late," Gracie Close called from behind the front desk. She grinned when Shar shot her an exasperated look. "What's up?"

"Turtle rescue." Shar plopped her bag on the counter. "Store this suitcase for me, will ya? And where are they? I hope I didn't miss anything…not that those two really need my input. They've got this renovation under control and we all know it."

Gracie had recently been hired as the manager of the hotel by Shar and her sisters. None of them wanted the actual job of the day-to-day running of the family resort that they had taken over together. The idea of being stuck behind that desk all day made Shar cringe every time the thought crossed her mind. Cali, who was getting married in five days, was already stretched to the limit with promotions and plans to travel with her soon-to-be husband, world-famous artist Grant Ellington. And Jillian's head was on landscape and flowers outside, not indoors with the dealings of day-to-day resort business. And Shar's third sister was busy off in movie land and had firmly turned down joining up with her three sisters to take over the running of the family resort. So that left Shar to step into the running of the place and everyone knew that would be an absolute disaster. Shar didn't do confinement, schedules, and tied down anything. Nope, Gracie was a godsend and very wonderful at her job. She'd had glowing credentials and Shar could have kissed the woman the day she'd walked through the door after accepting the job.

"They need you. Whether you think so or not, they do. They've headed to the renovation wing to meet with the contractor. If you hurry, you won't miss much."

"Shoot, I should have stayed at the hospital longer."

Gracie laughed. "Hurry, they're waiting."

Shar sighed and added unenthusiastically, "Thanks."

"You're very welcome."

Gracie's chuckles followed Shar as she hurried toward the double doors at the back of the lobby. Shar loved the resort that her family had owned for all of her life and the thought of selling it when her parents had decided to retire had prompted her and her two sisters to take it on. Her five brothers hadn't wanted the responsibility nor had Olivia and so, though Shar really couldn't see herself fully invested in the project, she'd stepped up to help Jillian and Cali. But sometimes she felt as if she were failing them. Not that they ever even hinted at it. But she felt it.

And yet, her heart was with her turtles and the volunteer hours she put in there. The job, however, didn't pay, thus she needed a job, a career—and the family resort was perfect.

She would do better. She would.

Hurrying to the back of the property, she walked past the gorgeous landscaped courtyard, due to Jillian's hands and planning. And then past the pool area with its fairly new mural painted by Grant Ellington, or McDreamboat as she called Cali's fiancé. The very idea of murals for the resort was due to Cali's marketing ideas. Shar loved the painting but she loved more the fact that McDreamboat had swept Cali off her feet. Shar had been all for the two of them getting together and had enjoyed watching their spark-filled romance—and doing a little egging on of it in her own big-mouthed way. But, she wasn't looking for that. Her sister Jillian had said they were all of the age that they were looking for love, but she was wrong. Shar loved her life and she was far from ready to give up her freedom of choice to a man. But she was thrilled for Cali.

Sometimes she wondered where she got such strong feelings on the subject and she really wasn't sure. All she knew was that like many of her five brothers, she was satisfied being single. But her sisters were meant for love and she'd give them a push when needed; it just wasn't for her.

Sexy Beach Guy popped into her thoughts. The man had nearly taken her breath away when he'd come out of that water, dripping wet and in nothing but his swim trunks.

Goose bumps prickled across her skin even now—he had been something to behold with that gleaming, muscled chest and taut abs. But it had been the scruffy jaw and raw look in his pale-blue eyes that had her toes curling in the sand—even as worried for the turtle as she'd been.

Shaking off the overwhelming walk down memory lane, she reached the open door of the room where renovations were set to begin. She peeked inside and instantly Cali saw her.

"Shar, you made it—what happened to you?" Cali asked, as Shar moved into the room still wearing her jogging outfit that was dirty and a bit bloody from the turtle's bleeding wounds.

"I'm sorry, but I had a turtle rescue this morning while I was out on the beach. I had to call the ambulance and well, it set me back from changing and showering." She caught a visual of herself in the mirror and grimaced. "Yikes, that's bad. As you can tell, I did not look in a mirror." Her hair looked like a mangled mess.

Her expression rapt, Jillian hurried over to her. "It's okay. You *saved a sea turtle*. That's incredible. You are so dedicated it hurts."

Shar laughed. "Thanks. I'll take saving a turtle over my appearance any day. So what's going on?"

"This is Abe Timmons, the contractor doing the

renovation."

Abe Timmons was a handsome man of about thirty to thirty-five, with smoky brown eyes that had smile lines creasing around the edges as he smiled at her. "Nice to meet you." He held out his hand.

Shar placed her hand in his and shook. "No, the pleasure is mine. I'm excited about this renovation. Glad to have you on board." She placed her hands on her hips and her thoughts went to the feel of the sexy man's touch earlier on the beach. Abe was a striking man, rugged, with an engaging smile that she was sure turned most women's hearts to jelly. Not hers. Nope, nothing—especially next to the fireworks that had exploded at the sexy man's touch. *And the eyes—oh wow, just a look from them—*

"Shar, are you okay?" Cali's question cut through her thoughts.

"Um, yes, sorry. Sure." She focused on Abe. "So, whatcha think about our plans?"

"I think it's very doable. Ripping out this wall and enlarging the bathrooms will steal space from the bedrooms but it'll still give you room for everything and make it more to the liking of people today. Nothing says outdated like a tiny bathroom."

"That's true," she said. "Windswept Bay Resort is about forty years old."

"And no major remodeling ever done," Cali added.

"Exactly," Shar agreed. "So it sounds good to me. What about you, Jillian?"

"Please let's do this. Knock it out," she laughed.

"It's a go, Abe," Cali said. "Let's do this. You have a green light."

"Then I'll have my crew start setting up in three weeks."

"That sounds perfect," Shar said. "We have a wedding happening soon and a honeymoon to be taken by Cali and she needs to be here when you get started."

"Congratulations. I read that in the papers," Abe said.

Cali blushed. "Thank you."

Jillian nodded at Abe and gave a small smile. "Yes, thank you."

"You're welcome," he said and Shar thought she

caught interest in his gaze when he looked at Jillian.

*Interesting.*

A few minutes later, he left and Shar stared at her sisters. "He seems like he'll be good. And he's cute, don't you think, Jillian?"

Jillian looked perplexed. "Yes, are you interested?"

"I just thought I saw interest coming from you."

"Not my type," Jillian said—a little too quickly, Shar thought. "But, Levi recommended him, so our big brother must trust him."

"And if the chief recommends him, then I think we're probably doing okay," Shar added.

Their brother Levi, the chief of police on Windswept Bay, had given his friend rave reviews. "Don't you agree, Cali?"

"Hmm, oh, yes I think so," Cali said, all smiles. "I'm sorry. My mind went to wedding plans."

*Of course they did.* She had been floating on cloud nine and distracted ever since she and Grant had decided to get married.

Shar laughed. "We've got to get you through this

wedding and back from your honeymoon so you'll get your mind back on the job."

"Sorry, I can't help it."

"And that is just the way it should be," Jillian said softly.

"So true." Shar could only imagine how her sister was feeling and to her this should be normal. "Now that we have that settled, you can completely focus on the wedding."

"That is what I plan to do. I never thought it was possible for me to want this again, but I am so very ready to become Grant's wife."

Shar saw the love there and was happy for her older sister. She had even been part of pushing Cali to step out and take a chance on love. "It's going to be a great night."

"It's going to be a very busy week," Jillian said. "I am so ready. You two just make me smile watching you. And I'm so happy for you both."

Cali was all smiles. "It'll be good to have us all together on Friday night too."

"I can't wait," Jillian said. "I think Olivia is

arriving Friday morning. It will be so good seeing her."

Olivia hadn't been home in a few months.

"Now that we've gotten that all settled, if it's not a problem, I'm going to run home and take a shower and put on a smidge of makeup. I'm going to drop by the hospital to check on Don Juan and then I'll be back."

"Wait." Cali laughed. "You *named* him *Don Juan?* Is he one great-looking turtle or something?"

"You know the person who finds an injured sea turtle gets the honor of naming it," Shar pointed out with a laugh. She had named it on a whim; she just hadn't thought about the consequences of naming the turtle after the sexy guy.

"So," Cali urged. "Why did you name it Don Juan?"

"Yes—we all want to know," Jillian joined in.

"It was the guy helping me rescue him."

"Really?" the sisters both asked in unison.

"Okay, so if you must know, I had help rescuing the turtle this morning and he was this amazingly gorgeous guy who came jogging from the surf to help me. I couldn't even think when I first saw him, so when it came time to name the turtle, Don Juan is what came out."

"Now that sounds interesting," Cali said.

"But what is his name?" Jillian smiled curiously.

"I was busy with the turtle. I don't know what his name is."

"But," Cali gasped. "You know where to find him, right?"

Shar didn't add that he was staying right down the beach from her. "I think I can."

Cali was all smiles. "Do you want to?"

"Maybe. Just to thank him for what he did, you know."

"Right, certainly," Jillian agreed. "That would be the right thing to do, to thank him."

"Were you on the beach near your house?" Cali asked, her expression hopeful.

"Yes, actually. Why?"

"That's a little bit of a secluded area. I wonder where he came from?" Jillian looked thoughtful.

"Oh," Cali gasped. "I think I heard the Glass Castle had been rented out. Do you think he came from there?"

Shar thought about it. The Glass Castle was the island's nickname for the large beach house at the end of the beach. It had so many windows it almost appeared from the beach to be all glass. And from the other beaches that curved along the coastline, the house, while not visible during the day, became a glowing gold flash as the settling sun reflected off all the glass.

"You know, he went in that direction when he went for a knife. I was busy working with the turtle and didn't watch where he went. Maybe he's renting the place or works for someone who rented it."

"You should go by there and find out. He's your neighbor." Cali looked mischievous. "I'm going to enjoy this if you find him. With all the pushing and teasing you do to me and Jillian about finding a guy, this sounds like our time to push."

Shar frowned at her. "Do not get your hopes up on paying me back for pushing you toward Grant. You know you love me for it. Besides, you have a wedding to get ready for. No time for matchmaking."

"Ha, like you listened when I said that to you," Cali pointed out. "Right, Jillian?"

"Oh, so true." Jillian chuckled. "You like the guy, Shar. What's the problem?"

Now she wished she hadn't mentioned him. "I'm too busy for a relationship. With the resort and all my volunteer work—I don't want to be tied down and you both know it."

"Ha! You like him," Cali exclaimed.

"You're hedging." Jillian chuckled. "That's a gardener's joke, if you didn't get it. But it works here."

"I am not trimming bushes nor am I about to jump off into some relationship with a guy I just met on the beach. Even if he is tempting." *Why had she added the last part?*

"Then maybe there's hope," Jillian added, her eyes bright.

"Hope for what?" Grant asked from the doorway.

"Of Shar falling for a tall, dark, and handsome stranger."

Shar shook her head at McDreamboat. "They are just teasing. Ignore them and take my sister to lunch so she'll have something more exciting than me to yap about."

Grant wrapped his arm around Cali when she crossed to give him a hug. He bent his head and kissed her soundly. "Your sister is right," he murmured after a moment. "I came to sweep you off your feet for lunch."

Shar watched the love in Cali's eyes and in Grant's for Cali. For a brief moment, she wished for that...but no, for her it would cost too much. But, as she headed back out to her car a few minutes later, she could not deny that she wanted to find out more about the sexy stranger.

His name, for starters.

# CHAPTER THREE

The following morning, after having helped save the sea turtle and meeting the woman he hadn't been able to get off his mind, Gage was not enjoying the moment as he stood on the deck and listened to his assistant talking on the other end of the phone line.

He rubbed the tension between his eyebrows as she talked. He hadn't slept well, and had given himself every argument he could find for why pursuing Shar was a bad idea. But he kept coming up short on how to stop himself from going after something...someone...he wanted.

And he wanted her—wanted to get to know her.

He was supposed to be reevaluating his life. He was taking account of his life, trying to figure out why, after losing his dad, he felt suddenly like a ship lost at sea. He was not here to get involved with a woman. But at the moment, that was exactly what he was planning to do.

At last, he broke in on Kym's lengthy dialogue of all the things that were waiting on him to handle back in his and his father's office. His office now. His alone.

"Kym," he said. "I'm just taking some time off. If the new acquisition can't wait a few weeks, then it's their loss. I'm fine without it. Tell them that. Do not tell them where I am and we'll go from there. And that goes for everything else. Keep the place running. I'm putting everything on autopilot and into your capable hands."

"But they're calling—"

Irritation coiled and snapped. "Tell them I just lost my father and they're just going to have to wait. Can you do that?" He was instantly sorry, but Kym had been with him long enough that she sometimes pushed more than she should. She forgot that he was the one in charge and she was there to do what he wanted her to do.

There was a pause. "Yes, I can do that," she said, all business now.

"Good. No one is to know where I am. And I don't know how you found this place but I like it here."

"I won't tell anyone. You know you can trust me, Benjamin." She used Gage's first name, the name his father had insisted he use in the business world.

He sighed. "I know. I didn't mean it that way. I'll talk to you later," he added and hit End. He refrained from tossing it out into the ocean; instead, he pocketed his phone and then walked around to his car. Moments later, he was driving down the winding road along the coast toward town. The top was down; the salt air whipped through his hair and helped relax him just a bit. That air smelled like freedom. And escape…and both were what he was looking for right now.

From an early age, he'd been taught by his father how to acquire businesses and industries that were in trouble. He'd been doing it most of his life. But, recently he'd lost his father and suddenly he was very aware of how short life could be. Milton Lancaster had been in the prime of his life at the age of fifty-nine when he'd died of a sudden and fatal heart attack. Gage had felt numb since it had happened.

But keeping to the pace his father had instilled in him, Gage had continued with business up until the funeral and then, immediately after he buried his dad, he left the funeral on his private jet for London and a contract negotiation waiting there for the company. It was just as Milton Lancaster would have wanted it…

But then, he'd not been able to go through with the meeting and had headed home. Something had come over him and he'd known he needed some time alone. So he'd made the call and had Kym find him a place to disappear for a few days. And now, here he was, staring at the outside of the Windswept Bay Sea Turtle Hospital and feeling fairly rebellious in his attitude. He'd do what he wanted and forget the rest, at least for a while.

Standing there, it happened, like it had yesterday

morning while meeting Shar and helping rescue the sea turtle: his adrenaline kicked in. It felt good as it hummed through him. He grabbed the door handle and then strode inside, hoping he'd find Shar on the other side of the door.

The room he entered held several rows of chairs that were set up in front of a large-screen TV. Pictures of turtles hung on the wall, as well as a huge shell.

"Hey man, good to see you." One of the guys from yesterday morning came into the room from the back.

Gage remembered his name was John and he held out his hand. "John, right? I thought I'd drop by and check on the patient. How's he doing?"

John grinned. "Great, considering how sick he was. Come on back and see for yourself."

Gage followed John through the door and into an open area with exam rooms on one side with glass windows much like those in an intensive care unit at the hospital. There was also one room that, guessing from the equipment in the room, was for surgery. He spotted the large turtle on a gurney in the room across from the operating room. IVs were hooked up to him and his flipper was wrapped in bandages.

"Ole Don Juan is making it but he's one lucky turtle to have been found by Shar when he was. We had to amputate much of his flipper to save him from the infection spreading further. And he's on massive amounts of antibiotics right now."

"Will he be able to survive? And with just a partial flipper?"

"He will, but more than likely he'll be a permanent resident here." John checked the monitors and then turned back to Gage. "You did good. Shar said you saved the day by coming along, then going and getting a knife to help her. The woman thinks she's Superwoman and if you hadn't come along when you did, she might have chewed the line off the turtle."

Gage chuckled at that. "Yeah, I got the impression that she's really passionate about saving turtles."

"Oh, that's the understatement of the year. Yes, she is. But then, we all are. You want to see the place?"

"Sure. It looks like you have a real operation going on here." Gage had never been in a place like this. Then again, he'd never really given sea turtles any thought at all other than that they were an interesting part of marine life.

John looked around. "We do. We rescue a lot of turtles up and down the coastline. Many of them have injuries and digestive issues that make them vulnerable to danger if put back into open water; therefore, they remain with us here. We have generous benefactors who help us keep our doors open. If not for them, we'd be in big trouble."

He led the way out the door and down a handicap accessible ramp. There were several large containers that looked like permanent above-ground pools.

"These are where we keep the turtles depending on the varying stages of their injury or illness."

"There are several different kinds, it looks like." Gage counted five different types in the first pool.

"Yeah, there are seven species of sea turtles and we see six of those in these waters. Loggerheads, Hawksbill, Kemp's Ridley, Green—you name them, there's a great chance we've got them. . Usually by the dozen. And six of the species are on the endangered species list."

"That's terrible."

"No kidding. We save as many as we can."

Gage looked around, taking in the facility and seeing the importance of it. "So where will Don Juan go after he's able to be moved into the water?"

"Back here." John led the way past several small buildings and into an area that had ten small cement above-ground holding tanks. Each one had a single turtle inside. Several were huge turtles and some were mid-sized.

Alex was there, studying one of the turtles. He said something to the young woman beside him and she left, giving Gage a smile as she passed him.

"So, you came to check us out." Alex held a clipboard, looked back at it and made a note and then looked back at the turtle again. He made another notation on the clipboard and asked without looking up, "So what do you think?"

"This is a great operation." Gage was really impressed with what they were doing. He saw several people working in different areas during his tour, looking as though they enjoyed the work.

"We're always looking for volunteers," John offered.

Alex moved to another turtle and started to examine it. "He's right. Anytime you have some free time, we'll put you to work."

The idea appealed to Gage. "I might take you up on that when I can. Does Shar work here?"

"Volunteers," John offered.

Alex focused on Gage, and he saw something flicker in Alex's eyes. His words were measured when he spoke. "She's a very important part of our program."

John nodded agreement. "That's the understatement of the year. That woman is passionate about saving as many sea turtles as she can. You saw her yesterday, making her morning jog along the coast. More than likely she was looking for new nests to mark. We try to protect the clutches."

"Clutches?"

"That's the egg group. We want the clutch of eggs to get to the hatching stage so there will be babies.

Shar is obsessed with saving baby turtles too."

Gage liked that. *When had he ever been obsessed with anything other than work? Something meaningful?* "She was really something," he murmured, and then realized he'd spoken out loud.

"Yes, she is." Alex asked, "I didn't catch your name yesterday—what is it? Are you living here or passing through?"

Gage wondered what her relationship was with Alex. There had been no ring on her finger; he'd taken note of that almost from the first moment he saw her. "I'm Gage." He caught himself before he said Benjamin Lancaster. "I'm Gage Lancaster. I'm staying on the island for a few days...maybe weeks. I'm finding it suddenly very...interesting," he finished, feeling suddenly territorial. From the appraising look he was getting from Alex, Gage was pretty sure the man had his sights set on the beautiful Shar. *Smart man.* But if there was no ring, then that meant at the moment there was an open door. And Gage's dad had taught him early on that an open door was made for walking through. In business, that meant if a company got sloppy and in over their head in debt, they left a door open and were ripe for a takeover. Not that in business he'd ever liked that part of Lancaster Industries, but it had been the part that got his dad out of bed, ready to go every morning. His dad had a killer instinct when it came to business. Gage hadn't and he'd known that most disappointed Milton. That being said, Gage knew how to get what he wanted when he wanted it...and today he wanted the beautiful, passionate Shar.

"Does she work around here?"

John looked from Alex to Gage, clearly sensing the territorial issues that hung in the air between them like a storm cloud. "Um, well, her family is the Sinclairs. They own the Windswept Bay Resort, and she and two of her sisters are running it now."

That was an interesting fact. Gage had passed the resort on his way to his rental the day he'd arrived. "Thanks. I'll drop by there then. I enjoyed the tour. All of you are doing great work here."

"Thanks. We have a great team." Alex watched him.

John agreed. "Come back anytime." He walked with Gage back the way they'd come. "We should have Don Juan in the water in a week or so. And there's more of the place to see. We have a saltwater pool for them when they're well."

"I'll be back."

Instead of leaving through the building, he took the sidewalk around the building and to his car. His steps were quick and his thoughts focused. He hadn't come to the island to hole up as he'd been doing the last few days. He'd come to escape for a while and to deal with the emotions of his dad's death that lay waiting and confusing behind a thin black curtain in his heart. But today, his thoughts were on a woman. Shar Sinclair. *And what a woman she was.*

He pressed the gas and pulled out onto the road in the direction of the resort.

The wind whipped through his hair and his shirt billowed open at the neck as the island air embraced him. And the vision of a girl inspired him.

# CHAPTER FOUR

It was nearly three o'clock on Tuesday when Shar closed her computer and stood. "I've worked on getting that group from Georgia set up and as far as I can see, they are good to go on arrival. And I've got to say it's a good thing, too, because I'm about at the end of my rope with Mrs. Albert Talbert the Third." She held up her fingers one at a time, counting. "One, two, three! I'm about struck out. If that little Southern woman says, 'bless your heart' to me one more time, I might just have to tell her to stick— Hey, you two, stop laughing. This is not funny." She glared at her sisters, who were not even trying to hide their laughter.

"Well, stop making all those mistakes," Cali chided her from behind the protection of her desk.

Shar scowled. "I'm not the one making the mistakes. That woman has called every day since she booked this shindig here and gotten some detail wrong. But still, *I'm* the one 'making' the mistakes." She put finger quotations around "making."

"Bless your little ole heart," Cali drawled, in a perfect imitation of Mrs. Talbert. "She blessed my heart a few times, too, when she first called about booking her gathering here. You're doing a great job, Shar. You have been polite and patient. And for that I'm proud of you."

Shar scowled deeper. "You act as if that's a shock. I can be patient and polite," she said, indignant. "If I want to be. And the truth is I'm this close," she pinched her thumb and pointer finger almost together, leaving only a slight gap, "to *not* wanting to be nice any longer."

"We could tell." Jillian chuckled.

"Well, sisters, I'm about to take a breather. I have

a plumber coming to the house to try and fix that leak I've had and I don't want to miss him."

"I thought you had someone come out last week to fix that," Jillian said.

Shar quirked a brow. "He canceled at the last minute. If I want water, I have to turn it on at the main water valve. And believe me, it's getting old."

"Why don't you have Horace come take a look at it?" Cali asked.

"Horace has his hands full keeping all the resort maintenance problems under control. I'll get this done, even if I have to do it myself."

Cali looked skeptical. "Good luck with that. Maybe you should call Dad or one of our many, many brothers. I'm sure one of them could do it for you."

Shar laughed at the inside joke. If there was one thing she did have, it was brothers and sisters. The Sinclair clan could make up their own baseball team. "I can handle my own business, thank you very much." She glanced at the clock. "I'm running late, though. Gotta go. Oh, and I'm picking our dresses up at ten in the morning. Woo-hoo!"

"I'm so excited," Cali said with joy in her voice. "And good luck with the plumber."

"Hope you picked a good one," Jillian called as Shar headed toward the door.

"Me too." Shar waved and then turned the corner and moved down the wide winding stairway that led to the lobby. She needed some fresh air and no Mrs. Albert Talbert calls for a while. She slowed midway down the stairs. A man stood in the lobby, studying Grant's mural.

Her heart skipped a beat—*okay, a lot of beats*—as she continued down the stairs and then toward the tall, very well-built man.

"Someone has connections," he muttered under his breath as she drew close.

Shar felt an unusual flutter of butterflies in her stomach. "My sister does."

He spun around and she almost gasped when those eyes she hadn't been able to forget bore into her. She lost her voice. *Who was she kidding—she couldn't breathe.*

"Hi," he said.

That simple word had her heart drumming again.

"I thought it was you." She smiled and hoped to goodness that he could not hear the racket her heart was making. "I thought I was going to have to hunt you down to thank you for helping me save that sea turtle yesterday morning."

"Oh really? Glad to know you were going to look for me. And I'm glad I could help. You were amazing. Fantastic, in fact." He held out his hand. "I came to introduce myself. I'm Gage Lancaster."

She took his hand and her pulse went into overdrive, just as it had the morning before. He didn't let go right away, just held her fingers in his for an extra beat. "You were pretty great yourself," she forced, trying to think of some dry response like she would normally make but nothing was there.

"I dropped by the hospital to check on the patient. John gave me a quick tour. It's a great place."

"It is. I love helping out there."

"So, your family owns this resort. And your sister has connections." He glanced at the mural. "They must be good connections to have gotten this."

Shar laughed. "Yes, two of my sisters and I run the resort. And my sister Cali has the connection. Grant is her fiancé. So you're a fan of Grant's?"

"I'd say that's a good connection." He smiled and Shar felt a little lightheaded. "Who couldn't be a fan? His work is inspiring."

She struggled to focus on what he was saying and not on her crazy uncharacteristic reaction to the man. "You'll have to see his two other murals that he did," she managed and then took a deep breath. "One is on the outside of the building facing the coastline. The other is next to the pool."

He rubbed his jaw and she so wanted to do that.

"Do you have time to give me a tour?"

"A what?" *Focus, woman—focus! And not on rubbing his jaw.*

"A tour of the place?" he clarified, looking hopeful.

And that single look tempted her to stand the plumber up right then and there. Yep, the plumber was lucky she even remembered him in that instant. And it was pure survival instinct on her part that had her remembering her leaky pipes. "Um, no. I...I have a thing," she admitted with great reluctance.

One perfect brown brow rose. "A thing?"

"Uh-huh." Her brows met. "Appointment. I have an appointment," she stammered.

"Then how about dinner?" he asked, without missing a beat.

"Dinner? No—no, I can't. I...I have plans tonight." Something in her, probably those survival instincts, told her to resist the overwhelming pull she felt toward the man.

He placed a hand on his heart. "I'm being brushed off."

He was cute *and* gorgeous. Shar laughed; that helped her persevere and feel more like herself. "No, really, I have previous plans." *But you could cancel...let the pipes leak for another day.*

She was so very tempted. "No," she said more firmly. "I can't."

He studied her, probably trying to decide whether he actually was being brushed off and she just didn't have the nerve to tell him.

"Are you and Alex together?"

*That came out of the blue.* "Alex? Um, no. Wait, I didn't mean it like that…I love Alex. He's a great guy, but no, I'm not with him."

"That's good to know. Just wanted to get that cleared up in my head. How about lunch tomorrow?"

"I'm sorry—"

"But you're busy."

"Well, yes."

"Dinner?"

"No." She bit her lip. "Look, I am sorry, but I can't. I hate to run but I need to go. I'm late. You should go see Grant's other paintings. Just follow the signs to the pool and then follow the path out to the beach and turn around. You can't miss it. Thanks again for helping save the turtle."

Shar felt a little sick to her stomach as she fled the building. *Why had she shut him out like that? Survival instincts be hanged!* Yes, she had legitimate plans but she could have explained them all. But…the truth was that looking into Gage Lancaster's eyes had suddenly scared her to death. It was as if she knew that if she started something with him, she might be in danger of falling into the deep end of the pool—and she wasn't sure whether she'd be able to swim or whether she'd sink.

Gage had just been blown off. He watched Shar flee. That was the only word that came to mind as he watched her exit the building. He'd never dated much. He'd been busy and most times women had been a complication when he had the pressure of helping build the empire his dad was so set on building. When he did ask a woman out, she usually jumped at the chance and she usually knew who he was. And that added its own complication. Manhattan was a long way away from Windswept Bay, though, and for the most part he was an unknown. At least so far.

"You're Benjamin Lancaster."

*So much for assumptions.* He turned to find a gorgeous, sleek woman in a see-through black cover-up that showed off a spectacular figure in a very skimpy black swimsuit.

"I am." He was tempted to deny his own identity.

She smiled a brilliant white smile. "I saw you on the cover of *Forbes*. I'm Gayle." She held out her hand. The diamond rings sparkled like the carats in her ears.

"It's nice to meet you, Gayle. I'm sorry, but I have to go. But it was nice meeting you."

"Likewise. I'm here all week." She batted false eyelashes at him.

"Ah, well, great. It's a beautiful island." He headed out the way Shar had just gone, making himself stride and not run. He caught a glimpse of her leaving in a yellow Jeep that had no top. Her dark curls waved in the wind as she goosed the gas and sped off down the road.

Unable to help himself, he jogged to his car and slid behind the wheel. Almost before he was in the seat, he had the engine of his sports car fired up. Glancing over his shoulder, he backed out, shifted into drive and pressed the gas pedal. His tires squealed as he goosed it to get on the road in front of three cars that would have cut him off from getting behind Shar if he hadn't had the powerful car.

He was bearing down on her when he came to his senses. *What was he doing? Had he lost his mind?* He lifted his foot off the gas and slowed; he pulled off the road and came to a jerking stop. He watched the yellow SUV disappear around a curve. He took a heavy breath. He had lost his mind. *What would she think if she found him chasing her down?* Not exactly the way to make a good impression. And he wanted to impress Shar Sinclair.

His phone rang and he pulled it out of his pocket to see it was Kym. He tossed the phone into the seat next to him. The next time he talked to her, he'd make the call. Right now, he had to figure out what his next move was on getting Shar Sinclair to spend time with him.

# CHAPTER FIVE

Shar's heart beat inside her chest like an out-of-control rock band as she sped down the road. She could not believe she'd left him standing in the middle of the resort.

*Gage.* She liked his name. It fit him. And he was more gorgeous than she'd thought. His blue eyes were intense—as was the way he'd looked at her. She tightened her hands on her steering wheel, remembering the way she'd reacted to his handshake. His touch was a bolt of heat that shot through her like a ball of fire. *And that look in his eyes.*

She shivered just thinking about it. Yep, those feelings were exactly what had her on the run.

She'd never felt that before...that thunderbolt. That heat. And she might be blunt sometimes and a little pushy—*okay, a lot pushy*—when she wanted something. But there was a part of her that was vulnerable. And all that emotion scared the daylights out of her. But she wasn't about to let anyone know that tidbit.

Nope, not her.

Arriving home, she pulled into her small garage and checked her watch. She was ten minutes late for the plumber and there was no plumber's van in sight. She sighed as she unlocked her door and entered the house.

"Rufus," she called, finding it unusual for her little Heinz 57 mixed dog not to meet her at the door. "Rufus, here, boy. Where are you?" she called again, half laughing. "Are you hiding?"

She walked into the kitchen and set her keys on the counter—and spotted two big footprints on her tile floor.

"No," she squealed and spun around, scanning the room for any sign of an intruder still being in the house. As she looked, she spotted the double doors onto her deck open. Her heart pounded in a completely different way than it had pounded moments ago upon seeing Gage. No, this adrenaline shot she could do without. She snatched up a heavy pan from the overhead pot rack and held it like a weapon as she moved around the end of the bar.

A note on the floor caught her attention. Scooping it up, she saw it was from her plumber. A quick scan had her growling in aggravation and frustration. She might just hurt Albert Meeks when she saw him. He'd arrived early, found an open door and just let himself inside. On top of that, he couldn't find her leak so he left. *So much for having an appointment with him.* And in the meantime, Rufus had escaped.

Her new little rescue pup was still skittish and had probably gotten out of the house and was hiding somewhere, frightened.

Jogging out onto her deck that overlooked the almost private beach, she hurried down the steps, calling Rufus's name. When he didn't answer with a quick bark or show himself, she began to really worry. She hurried back inside, grabbed his leash and then ran back out to look for him through the neighborhood.

She'd found him at the local shelter and could not leave him behind. He was so stinkin' ugly with his dull-brown, scruffy-haired body and large head. Ugly but cute fit him perfectly. She thought he was adorable and sweet. And she had to find him.

Shar raced out onto the beach, hating the idea of the poor puppy being lost. She looked down the beach both ways, hoping for some sign as to which way to start her search.

It was late in the afternoon and there was no one around. Shar loved this beach because it was so secluded. Most of the homes on this beach were owned by wealthy homeowners who vacationed here on occasion. This gave her the beach to herself much of the time but it also gave Rufus so many places to run and hide and no one to see him. The homes were not right on the beach, purposefully hidden among the landscape and quietly secluded. As she scanned the beach, deciding which way to go, the Glass Castle house caught her attention at the end of the beach. It was kind of an eyesore among all of the more sedate homes but she thought that was where Gage was staying. He'd headed that direction when he'd gone to get a knife. She headed that way.

"Rufus," she called. "Come here, boy." Over and over, she called for the pup as she went from one home to the other. It was taking forever. There were actually twenty homes hidden along this beach; no one would ever realize that until they'd walked up each path and hunted through bushes and sand dunes along the way. And she had done just that in the last hour with no sign of her little puppy.

Hot, in more ways than one, Shar decided she might very well hurt the plumber when she found him. First, he'd entered her home without permission, but the worst was he'd let her puppy escape. Yep, Meeks better stay hidden just as good as Rufus was if he knew what was good for him.

Pushing her anger aside, Shar headed toward the last home on the stretch of sand and prayed Rufus was there.

Gage was unloading groceries from his car when he heard a whimper from the bushes just outside the garage. He'd spent an hour at the grocery store after coming to his senses and discontinuing chasing Shar down in his car. Deciding he needed to act like a sane person and not some infatuated lunatic had been a good move.

The whimper came again. Gage set the bag of groceries on the hood of the car and went to investigate. Crouching down, he peered into the hedge. Two big, dark eyes blinked back at him.

"Well, hello there, little guy." Gage wasn't sure whether he'd ever seen such an ugly puppy but the poor thing shivered, he was so scared, and Gage's heart melted. "Come on, come out," he coaxed. When the pup made no move to do as he was asked, Gage eased his hands in and hoped he didn't get bitten. There was a lot of hair but as his hand wrapped around the body, the pooch was more fluff than meat and bone. Looking at the name tag attached to the collar, Gage smiled. "Okay, Rufus. Let's get you inside and call your owner."

Remembering his groceries and the cold stuff that needed to be refrigerated, Gage grabbed the bag off the hood and one-armed it into the kitchen as Rufus snuggled into the crook of the other arm.

He set the bag on the counter, and then opened the refrigerator and pulled milk, butter, and a few other cold items out of the bag and placed them on the shelf. Then he went back for the next bag. Rufus was content where he was and wasn't trembling as much as he had been, so Gage decided he'd get the groceries unloaded first and then he'd call the number on the collar. A few minutes later, he closed the fridge's door and then looked down to find Rufus asleep with his scruffy head propped on Gage's arm.

Grabbing the phone, he walked out onto the deck and sank into a chair. The now snoring dog rolled over in the crook of his arm and passed out, legs sprawled in all directions, belly up.

Gage laughed. "Why don't you relax, little buddy,

and make yourself at home."

He was dialing the number when he heard someone yelling. He paused pushing numbers on the keypad and looked around; Shar was coming down the beach.

"Rufus," she called. The word broke up in the breeze.

Gage shot out of the chair in instant reaction to seeing her. The movement woke Rufus; the pup jerked awake and barked as it scrambled to roll over in Gage's arms. Barely able to hang onto the suddenly overactive animal, Gage was laughing when Shar spotted him. She stopped in the sand and they stared across the expanse between them. His pulse was scrambling more than Rufus had been and instantly, he moved down the steps toward her. She took his breath away.

Rufus barked again and started to wiggle the moment he spotted her. And maybe it had been the wind, but it was apparent that until that moment Shar hadn't realized that Gage was holding her dog.

Now she noticed him and her eyes widened when

she spotted Rufus. Instantly, joy bloomed over her face and she sprinted the last little stretch of sand between them. Gage had never in his life believed he could envy a puppy but in this moment he did. He wanted Shar to see him, just him, and react with that much joy.

"You found Rufus!" Tears sprang to her eyes as she took the now squirming and barking pup from Gage's arms. "Sweet boy, you must have been so scared." She hugged the pup close and then lifted him up so she and Rufus were eye to eye. "I won't ever let that happen again. I promise." And then she hugged him close again.

Gage had been in many boardrooms and tough negotiation situations in his life and always had been able to take control of the situations with ease. But right then, in that moment, he was at a loss. He swallowed the lump lodged in his throat just as she lifted her misty green eyes to his.

"Where did you find him? I've been looking for over an hour."

"He was in the bushes beside the garage. I just got home and found him. I was dialing the number on his collar when you showed up."

"I'm just so grateful. I had a plumber coming today and I got here late but the plumber went inside my house without me and left the door open." Her eyes flashed that fire that he'd seen when she'd been trying to free the turtle. "Rufus is a rescue dog and as you can tell, he's very nervous. He ran and probably never looked back until he found just the right bush to hide in."

Gage smiled. "I'm glad it was at my house."

"Me too. But Mr. Meeks the plumber is not going to be so glad about anything after I pay him a visit tomorrow."

She had a temper but then, he didn't blame her for being mad. Rufus had been through a lot and something could have happened to him. "He let himself inside?"

"Yes. He found my back patio door unlocked but he left me a note and a few dirty footprints before he left."

Gage frowned. He didn't like the sound of Mr. Meeks at all. "I think you need to come inside or sit here on the deck and relax for a few minutes. I'll get you a drink. What would you like?"

She tapped her toe on the deck and snuggled Rufus against her neck—instantly Gage was thinking about placing kisses along her neck. He held back a groan. He was really in deep here.

"Coffee would be great if you have it."

He grinned. "A woman after my own heart. Sit right there and I'll bring it out. Or come in, if you'd like."

She looked thoughtful and then she nodded toward his house. "Actually, I've never been inside the Glass Castle. I'd love to see it."

"The what?"

She laughed. "The Glass Castle. That's what the locals have always called this place. There are so many levels and so much glass."

He looked up at the three different floors with an abundance of huge windows. "You're right. I can see what you mean. My assistant rented it for me." He held the door for her. "After you and Rufus." He scratched the pup's head as Shar brushed past him. It was all he could do to not take a strand of her dark hair in his fingers. *Okay, so he had officially lost his senses.* The woman was driving him crazy and she was doing nothing but being near him.

"So, is this beach always so deserted?" he asked to distract himself from focusing on Shar. He walked around the bar into the kitchen.

Shar moved to stand in the living room. Late afternoon sunbeams highlighted her through the window behind her.

"You rented a house in a very exclusive spot. The only reason I live in the neighborhood is because I live in the pool house of one of the homes. The older couple who own the house only come down 'sometimes' in the summers." She did air quotations with her fingers around sometimes. "They were looking for someone to watch over the place for them. They're donators for the sea turtle hospital, so when they mentioned it to me, I jumped at the opportunity."

"Sounds like a great arrangement." And lucky him—he really liked the arrangement. If he hadn't been at the grocery store, he might have seen her on the beach sooner.

"It is for me. Most of the people who own these homes visit every once in a while, so this stretch of sand is probably the quietest on the island. I can tell you that there is no one else staying in any of the homes right now. I've just spent time in all the shrubbery. It's a wonder someone's burglary detection system didn't rat me out."

He chuckled. "You're probably lucky."

"My brother would have been surprised to arrive with sirens blazing to find me in the bushes."

He paused putting coffee grounds in the coffee maker. "Your brother is a cop?"

"One of my brothers, Levi, is police chief." She set Rufus on the ground and the puppy eagerly raced around the room sniffing and checking things out. "I have five brothers."

He coughed. "Five. You have five brothers?"

She laughed and sank onto the barstool. "Oh yes, I do. And I have three sisters."

"Wow."

She laughed. "I'm used to that reaction. I love my

big family."

"I'm an only child so my upbringing was probably a lot more sedate than yours."

She snorted. "Oh, believe me, it was wild. Cam, our cowboy, was always roping someone and Jake, the daredevil turned scuba diver among other things, was always scaring my mom to death with his antics. And then there was Levi, now the chief of police, always pushing limits growing up and my other two brothers Trent and Max—so yes, it was very active. Plus me and my three sisters."

He digested the size of her family. "Let's give us a chance for a few minutes before calling them in. *Eight,*" he said as the number sank in. "You have eight brothers and sisters."

"Yes I do," she said with an emphatic nod of her head. "You don't have something against the number eight, do you? Or nine if you count me."

"No, I was an only kid so that's a big number to me. You must have had huge family gatherings."

She laughed. "Oh, we still do. I'm sure if you were the only kid then they were  way louder than yours."

"An understatement, I'm sure. I was actually going into the office with my dad pretty early on. My mother died while giving birth to me. A string of nannies raised me. At least they did until I was ten and drove the last one away. At that point, my dad started taking me to the office with him."

She looked sad. "I'm sorry about your mother. I can't imagine not having my mom."

"We made it work."

"After you ran off no telling how many poor nannies." She laughed. "I bet you were a terror."

"Hey, I take offense to that. I was a curious kid who wanted to spend more time with my dad, who tended to work all the time."

"So you knew what you were doing."

"I hoped I knew what I was doing. All I know is that when we were between nannies, I'd get to go to the office. It was like a magical place to me. I'd get to see my dad and the secretaries would get me anything I wanted. It couldn't be beat."

She studied him. "You were going to the office at

the age of ten. You're going to have to tell me more about that. It sounds awful. I'm twenty-six and if it wasn't for the fact that I was in an office with my sisters and they tend to let me do my own thing when I want to, I'd straight up go bonkers. Full-time office life is not for me."

He grinned at her and instantly her eyes narrowed. "What's so funny about that?"

"I think I'd already figured that out." She was not only gorgeous, spunky, and passionate...she was cute. It was irresistible. "I think you like running around wearing your superhero cape better."

She looked confused. "My what?" She then laughed.

The sound swirled in his chest and he was helpless against the force of it.

# CHAPTER SIX

"I think you're the local superhero. After talking to the guys at the hospital earlier today, I realized you didn't find Don Juan by accident. You were out turtle hunting, like you do often."

Shar swirled in his chest like a song playing over in his head.

"You were the hero on that one." She got a picture of him coming out of the surf and her mouth went dry.

"Hey, I just helped. You were the hero and from what Alex and John told me today, you make searching for and protecting sea turtles a daily endeavor. And it looks like you rescue pups too."

Feeling uncomfortable with the high praise, Shar stood. "I just want to help them."

He held her gaze and she was warmed by his praise. "I think I'll take my pup and head home now."

"But what about coffee?" Gage came around the bar. "I wish you'd stay. I was about to make dinner. And you haven't looked at the house. I sound desperate," he said and looked a little sheepish. "I actually am. I know earlier you said you had other plans but, I don't know anyone in town and I thought, now that you know me a little better, that maybe your plans could be changed."

*Oh, how they can be.* Shar tried not to listen to the wistfulness of her inner voice. "Well, to be honest, the plumber was my big date. And he blew me off *and* let my dog out, so the date hasn't exactly been all I had hoped for."

He laughed at her humor. "I guess not."

"And dinner was going to be a peanut butter sandwich and a glass of water, if you must know."

*So it hadn't been with a boyfriend.* Gage's mood

hefted up a major mountain. "Then let me save you from the sandwich and hope we can salvage your day. What do you say?"

"You've already done that because you found Rufus."

"Then reward me with your company for dinner."

"Ha! I don't know how much of a reward that will be, but you're on."

"Perfect. I have to warn you that I'm not the best cook but I can manage a few things. However, there are no guarantees that we might not have to resort to peanut butter—except that I don't have any in the house."

She smiled broadly. "We'll manage. And I'll fess up that my skills aren't great but I bet we can figure it out between the two of us."

Gage fought the urge to take her in his arms and tell her that he thought the two of them together could figure a lot out. Instead, he forced himself to move back into the kitchen. "I'm thinking we've got this covered."

She shot a smile at him. "Thinking positive. I like

it." She walked into the kitchen and turned on the water, and then washed her hands. "Just a piece of advice: don't 'bless my heart' about anything and we'll be okay."

He laughed. "Sounds like there's a story there."

"Oh yes, there is."

"Then out with it. I'm all ears."

# CHAPTER SEVEN

An hour later, with the scent of chicken Alfredo simmering in the oven, Shar looked around and laughed. "Wow. I just can't get over the mess we've made. This looks like the first time all of my brothers and sisters and I decided to fix Mom breakfast for Mother's Day. It took her two days to get it cleaned up."

He picked up a dirty pan before she could. "She must be something to have raised that many kids."

Shar sighed. "She's the best. But...I don't know. I sometimes wonder what she would have done with her life if she hadn't had so many kids. Her entire life was built around my dad and us. Still is, for that matter." She held her hand out for the pan but he didn't give it to her.

"Do you think she regrets it?" He moved to place the pan under the running water.

His arm brushed hers and sent a shiver of delight and electricity sparking through her. "Oh, no, I didn't mean it that way." She tried not to let the way he made her feel cause her to do or say something ridiculous... *Kiss me...now, would be nice.* She ignored the pestering voice in her head and opened the dishwasher.

"No, I'll do this." He reached around her to place the pan in the top rack of the dishwasher. The movement had him very close. Her rampaging heart kicked against her ribcage.

He let his gaze roam over her face and that only kicked her heart into the stratosphere. The clock on the wall sounded as if it were on loudspeaker as it was the only sound in the room.

And then he wrapped his arms around her.

Instantly Shar's blood rushed through her at the

explosive speed of a rocket launching into space. She couldn't breathe as she looked into Gage's baby-blue eyes. His arms were strong around her.

"I've been wanting to hold you close since the first moment we met."

"Oh," she breathed shakily as his blue gaze shifted from her startled gaze to her lips. Her knees melted like butter in a microwave. *Oh, my...* Shar didn't get shook up; she didn't...but she was...

"You're beautiful, you know," he murmured and then he lowered his head and kissed her.

*Oh, oh...* She sighed as her arms went around his neck automatically. His kiss was powerful, like crashing waves slamming down and then washing onto shore only to recede again into the next wave. Shar's fingers curled into his shoulders as he stepped closer, backing her up against the kitchen counter as he deepened the kiss. All there was in that moment was the feel of his lips against hers and the strength of his embrace as she kissed him back with enthusiasm...but suddenly the crashing waves she felt were real as warm water poured over the side of the sink and drenched her.

She yelped, and then laughed as she broke the kiss. "The dish water." She laughed, pulling away from Gage, and reached for the faucet.

Gage burst into laughter too and grabbed a handful of dishrags from a drawer and bent to clean up the water.

"We just thought we had a mess." He laughed, crouching down to begin sopping up the water.

While he cleaned up the floor, Shar reached down into the soapy water and found the drain. She couldn't stop laughing. "Nothing like getting doused with water to kill a moment." She laughed. *Or a fire.*

"Sorry about that." He looked up from where he crouched, wiping the floor. "You're soaking wet." He jumped up and headed out of the kitchen. "Hang on, I'm getting a towel."

She wiped the counter while she waited, glad to have a moment to pull herself together. He had a fluffy white towel in his hands when he came back into the room. He handed it over with a smile.

"I'm really sorry."

"It's okay." She took the towel and wrapped it

around her waist. "I'll dry before you know it."

"I could get you a pair of my warm-ups. They'll be big on you but you'd be dry."

"No, really, I'll be fine. This towel will have me dry as can be in no time." Feeling more unnerved than she was used to, Shar clung to the towel as if it were a life preserver.

He studied her with a perplexed look. "If you say so. Let's eat on the deck—that'll help, too."

"Great idea."

"And when we're done, I'll walk you home and then I'll come back and do the dishes." He chuckled as he took the casserole out of the oven and set it on the stovetop. "I have to say that this smells delicious. I think we might not have to eat your peanut butter tonight."

Shar knew that at that moment it didn't matter what they ate; she wasn't going to taste anything because all she was thinking about was Gage and the feel of his lips on hers.

A few minutes later, they each carried plates out to the

patio, with Rufus trailing them. He pranced out to the edge of the deck and stared out at the ocean.

"Don't even think about running off." Shar set her plate on the table. As if knowing she was speaking to him, he turned his bushy head her way and cocked his ears. "Yeah, you know I'm talking to you."

"Does he run off often?" Gage sat down across from her.

"No. I haven't had him but two weeks. But he's never run off. I think today a stranger came in and either he ran off right then or while the plumber was in there, he hid and when he left, Rufus found the door open and went exploring."

"I bet he realized soon after he was lost that he wanted you back."

Rufus came over to where she was, sat down on her foot and watched the ocean from that vantage point. Shar felt a tug at her heart and reached down to gently rub his ears. "I know I wanted him back. It scared me. In all honesty, I don't put myself out there that much. He's the first pet I've had in a very long time."

"Really? I would have thought you had a lot of them."

She shook her head and toyed with her salad. "No. I had a cocker spaniel in high school and I loved her dearly. It hurt far too badly when she died. I've never been able to let myself actually have an animal of my own ever since that time."

He looked confused. "You really loved her."

"Dolly. I loved Dolly so much. And I've just never wanted to feel that again. I understand that I'm going to lose people I love sometime in the future. And I can't stop that. But I don't have to ever go through that with an animal. And so I have rescue programs I send animals to. But then I saw Rufus and he needed someone."

"And you rescued him for yourself."

"Something about Rufus was undeniable. I knew we belonged together."

They ate in silence after that, listening to the waves and feeling the soft breeze.

"Have you ever felt like you and a man belong together?"

The question had her taking a drink of her tea. "No," she managed to say and hoped it sounded convincing. Because the truth was that she had that feeling about Gage. And she barely knew the man.

But then, she'd only taken one look at Rufus and she'd known the truth.

"So what are you doing here?" Shar asked later, after they'd finished their meal and Gage was walking her home.

The moon was out and it sparkled on the water like a spotlight from heaven; Gage felt the magic of the evening. He'd never dreamed this morning when he'd set out to the sea turtle hospital in search of Shar that the day would end with him having had dinner with her and now walking along the moonlight beach where they'd met.

"Can you hear that?" he asked, deliberately not answering her question. "It sounds like music." He paused and listened to the waves and the wind; somewhere from one of the homes along the beach came the distinct sound of wind chimes. They mingled with the sounds of the ocean and wind and created a romantic symphony.

"I call it a Windsong." She stopped to listen.

He studied her. "I like it."

"Me too. It's like nature's love song."

He smiled at her and fought the desire to pull her into his arms. "I like that more."

"So," she said slowly, eyeing him as he took a step toward her. "Why are you here on our island? Vacation?"

"No, I'm hiding out." It was the truth.

"From?"

"My life, I think." She probably thought he was crazy.

"And why would that be?"

"My father died eight days ago."

"Oh," she gasped. "I'm so sorry. You have my condolences."

He realized in that moment that he'd been hiding from all of it: his dad's dying, the life he'd been groomed for, the life he'd never lived. And as he looked at Shar, he found himself thinking of possibilities of a life he'd never dreamed of...one with her. He knew that was completely irrational thinking but that was what he was thinking and there was no stopping it.

"Thank you." He studied her, unable to take his eyes off her. "My father was all about the work. Always going from one big deal to the next. As far as I know, he never slowed down. And I kept up the pace. I hopped on the company plane right after the funeral and I flew to London, where business associates were waiting for me to seal a deal. But I ended up having the plane fly me back to the States and had my assistant find me a place to disappear for a few days. Or weeks."

"And here you are. Right where you need to be. You needed time off after your dad's death. I can't believe you left the day of his funeral and flew overseas. You needed a break. Time to grieve." Her eyes flashed.

"And you sound like you know what you're talking about."

"I lost my grandmother last year and it was hard to do anything for days. We were really close. Grief takes time."

He raked a hand through his hair. "Yeah. I just thought carrying on as he would have wanted me to was the way to go."

"I think carrying on the way you needed to is and was the way to go. And Windswept Bay is a laid-back place to retreat and get your heart healed."

"I believe you're right." He started to walk again and she walked beside him. Rufus raced ahead of them and then raced back to them and circled them before heading off after a lapping wave.

"This is me." She pointed to lighted windows and they headed across the sand toward the light. "So, who exactly are you, Gage?" she asked when they reached her porch.

"I'm just a guy who works in corporate America."

She studied him. "No—who are you?"

He wanted to be honest with her but would knowing who he was make a difference in how she perceived him? How she reacted to him? There were scores of women who came after his name, his money and looked at him as a commodity. He'd felt that at the resort with the woman in the lobby; he'd already forgotten her name. He'd never forget Shar's name.

"I'm Benjamin Gage Lancaster of Lancaster Industries."

"Lancaster Industries sounds familiar."

"It makes the news every once in a while."

Shar studied him. And now he wished maybe he hadn't told her.

Her eyes widened. "Got it. You were on the cover of one of those financial magazines," she gasped. "I didn't read it, but I noticed your picture."

"I did an interview with them."

"You didn't have a five-o'clock shadow in the picture on the cover?" Her eyes twinkled in the moonbeam.

He laughed, feeling the tension ease a little. "No, clean-shaven all the way and knotted up inside business suits and dress shoes. I bought what clothing I have with me at a store in the airport. All the way down to the flip-flops and boat shoes."

"So that explains the *I love Florida* T-shirt."

He plucked at his shirt. "So you don't like palm trees and Florida?"

She smiled. "Oh no, I love it." Her smile faded. "So you just lost your father? I'm sorry. I can't imagine a world without mine in it. What happened to him?"

His hand tightened on the deck railing. So that was it; she just breezed past the *Forbes* article and went straight back to sympathy for his loss. An unexpected lump formed in his throat. He had to clear his throat before he spoke. "He had a massive heart attack in a business meeting. He died instantly. I buried him three days later."

"I'm sorry. What was he like?" she asked gently and smiled encouragingly.

Her question threw him a little. "He...he was a powerful man, competitive. Driven. He taught me everything I know. He was very successful."

"I've figured that one out." She studied him with an odd look in her eyes. "You just talked about him in business terms. What was he like when he wasn't working?"

"He worked all the time. He taught me to work all the time." He didn't miss the shadows that came into her eyes. "Like I said, I left his funeral and flew to a closing overseas. It's what he would have wanted but I ended up coming straight back to the States for time alone."

"Good for you. You must be hurting. Grieving. You should never have been working in the first place."

"I had commitments. My father was a stickler for keeping commitments."

"Your father died. You're entitled to mourn."

He stared at her; she'd echoed in similar ways what he'd told Kym. "It's more than that, though. I realized that I don't want to live my life where all that matters is work and commitments to work. I've never taken a vacation. I've been to some of the most beautiful places in the world but I've looked at it from behind a glass hotel room window, a car window, and a conference room window." He turned to face her. "And then I meet you. You're passionate about something and you're vibrant and alive and caring."

She stood on the top step and he was one step below her, making them eye to eye. He reached for her and she came hesitantly at first into his arms. "You draw me to you like nothing I've ever felt before." His adrenaline raced with the feel of her in his arms. He knew he was moving too fast but he'd never felt as passionate about anything in his life as he did about Shar. And it was hard to hold back.

She placed her arms around him and hugged him tightly. He felt her heart thundering against his. He just held her. They stood like that for a long moment with the sound of the ocean behind them and the moonlight surrounding them.

After a moment, she pulled out of his arms. "You've never had a vacation?"

"Never. Until now."

"That's just sad. We'll have to do something about that. I have an early morning and a busy day tomorrow. What are you doing at five-thirty in the morning?"

He narrowed his eyes. "I don't know—why?"

"I look for turtle nests at various places every morning. I try to go at sunrise before too many other people are stirring. You can come, if you want?"

"I want," he said without hesitation. He pulled her back into his arms and then lowered his lips to hers. The taste of salt air on her lips was a reminder that he was in a tropical place on a magical night. He made the kiss quick, not trusting the emotions that threatened to overwhelm him.

"You have a good night," he said, his voice husky.

She nodded and backed out of his arms, turning to the door. She pulled a key from her pocket and had the door opened quickly. Rufus raced inside as if he was overjoyed to be back at his place.

"Gage." She turned back to him. "I'm not looking for a relationship. Nothing serious."

Her words didn't surprise him. He'd felt that about her. And understood it to a point, he thought. He cupped her jaw. "One day at a time," he said. "I'll see you in the morning."

He left then, heading back the way they'd come. Not giving her the chance to say more.

# CHAPTER EIGHT

Shar couldn't think straight as she watched Gage disappear across the sand. Every fiber of her body hummed a happy tune from the kisses that he'd given her and she could still feel the last one. Her fingers went to her lips automatically, as if touching her lips where he'd kissed her would hold onto the feelings he'd drawn from her.

She wasn't on the market for a relationship. She wasn't.

*But...could she stop what he made her feel?*

Locking the door, she forced herself to stop

watching the beach where he had been and she headed to her room to get ready for bed.

He'd lost his dad and he'd never been on a vacation, despite all the money he obviously had. There was more to life than just work.

Her own father had worked long hours at the resort when she was growing up but he'd always had time for her and her brothers and sisters. There was a balance and it was obvious Gage's dad hadn't had that. And neither had Gage.

The entire idea threw her into a tailspin and she'd been unable not to invite Gage to her early morning excursions. She could tell that he might not realize it but he was in need of some life. And she couldn't help showing him what he'd been missing. She liked to rescue things...and she couldn't help the feeling that Gage Lancaster needed rescuing.

The fact that he attracted her like nothing she'd ever felt was an exciting addition that she also couldn't ignore. She'd just have to let him know up front that she was not one to get tied down.

Nope. Not her. And yet there was no denying that

she couldn't wait till sunrise.

When Shar pulled up outside Gage's home the next morning, he was waiting on the front porch of the massive house. He jogged toward the car and her heart skipped beats...she'd anticipated seeing him even in the short hours that she'd managed to sleep.

"I've been waiting for hours to see you again." He slid into the seat next to her and before she could react, he'd leaned across and kissed her soundly on the lips.

A protest formed in the back of her mind but the exhilaration of his touch buried it behind the haze of joy that filled her. "It was a short night," she managed as he relaxed back in the seat and smiled at her.

"Too long if you ask me," he said. "I'm ready for the sunrise with you."

Shar was not often at a loss for words but she was now. Not finding a coherent reply, she drove. Finally, words seeped into her thoughts. "It's going to be a beautiful sunrise. I can guarantee it. We're going to one of my favorite beaches on the opposite side of the island. We get sunsets on this side; we get sunrises on the opposite."

"Sounds good to me. Is it far?"

"Nothing on the island is far." She began to feel more herself as she drove.

"I'm starting to realize that. It's not like Manhattan. Of course, a cab can get you where you want but it's never a straight, easy shot in traffic."

She laughed. "I've never been to New York. Not sure I'd like it."

"It's certainly different than here but it has its charm. You'll have to come visit sometime. I'll show you everything."

She looked across at him. "Does that mean you're going to slow down and enjoy yourself a little more than you have in the past?"

He looked thoughtful. "I've given it some thought and I'm going to make some changes."

For some reason she wasn't quite sure about, his words made her sad and happy at the same time. "Good. I'm glad."

"But right now I'm going to enjoy the sunrise and

searching for clutches with you."

Those words caused a whirlwind in the pit of her stomach. "Sounds good. And well deserved."

As they arrived at the beach, the thin pink line of sunrise was just beginning to peek over the horizon. She parked her car. "Let's grab the gear and head out," she said.

"Lead the way." He joined her at the back of her vehicle.

Within moments, they were jogging along the water's edge toward the rising sun. The gentle waves lapped just a few feet from them. Gage's stride was longer than hers but he paced himself with her.

"I just watch for turtle trails coming from the water. You usually can't miss them. And then we mark the area with the eggs. It warns curious people to stay away."

She'd pulled on her backpack today that held small flags and yellow tape warning people to stay back. She'd made the mistake of not wearing her backpack on her own beach and had needed her knife that day.

"So you do this every morning?"

"Every morning. I need exercise and so the two hobbies go together well."

"Multi-tasking at its best." He grinned. "Hey, there." He pointed to tracks ahead of them in the dim morning light.

"Yes, that's what we're looking for," Shar said, happy he'd spotted it first. She'd been slightly distracted by him. "I had a feeling today would be a good day."

"So you don't find them every day?" he asked.

She pulled off her backpack and pulled out a couple of red flags and handed them to Gage. "Take these and we'll push them into the ground on either side of the hole. No, there's not enough of me to go around. But someone finds them and calls them in. I just enjoy the thrill of finding them myself."

He laughed. "I totally get it."

She heard the excitement in his voice and she felt that he did get it. Not everyone who'd ever been in her life had felt the same way.

She pulled out a notebook and noted where the nest was and then from where they stuck out of the backpack, she pulled out three wooden sticks each eighteen inches long. She handed these to Gage too. Last, she pulled out a flyer that cautioned people to stay back and not to touch the sea turtle nest.

Within seconds, they had three stakes in the ground around the nest and then the caution tape was attached from one stick to the other so that it made a protective barrier.

"And so our work is done. And just before the sun comes up."

Gage picked her backpack up and strapped it on his back. "I'll carry this for you. I had actually forgotten about the sunrise." He smiled.

"Me too. Come on."

She jogged a short distance to a flat rock big enough for two. "I love to watch the sunrise from here."

They sat beside each other on the rock, arms brushing. They were barely touching and yet Shar had never felt so attuned to anyone in her life.


"I had a blast," Gage said later, as he got out of the car in front of his house.

"I did too. You helped a creature that's struggling with extinction today. Every one that we can save is one more to carry on."

He got that. Not until he'd seen the eggs had it hit him, though. "I get what you're doing, Shar. I could get hooked on it too."

She smiled over at him. Excitement sparkled in her eyes and he understood it now, the determination she had and the exhilaration she felt when she found a nest.

He could become obsessed with that feeling himself. He wondered whether that was how his father felt in business. Gage had never felt that kind of all-consuming drive and passion...until he'd met Shar. Until he saw her passion and he wondered what it would feel like to have that passion directed at him. Someone was going to be a lucky man one day. Shar Sinclair was a special woman.

"I'll see you later. Have a good day at work."

She'd told him that she jogged and looked for sea turtles eggs early and then showered and headed by the hospital to check on the turtles; then she headed to work by nine.

She and her sisters had decided earlier that year to take over the running of the resort so their parents could retire. And they were doing some remodeling to the over property.

"It's going to be busy. I'm picking up bridesmaids' dresses from the cleaners. The wedding is here and I can't believe it."

"Your sister and Grant?"

"Yes. You're very welcome to come to the party. We're having the wedding on the beach of the resort but there will just be family and a few close friends of the family. But then we're opening the reception up to the resort guests and friends."

"It sounds like a fun time. I'd hate to intrude."

"Believe me, you won't be. There's a lot going on behind the scenes and there will be press there and photographers taking shots for advertising purposes, along with the regular wedding photographer. It was the best way we could come up with a solution to promote the resort without inviting the whole world to Cali and Grant's wedding. We're just hoping no helicopters show up."

He laughed, and then realized she was serious. "I guess Grant is the reason for that?"

"Hey, it could be my sister or the resort," she teased indignantly. "But it's not. It's Grant. Cali has had to adjust to the idea."

"I bet."

"Come by when you have time and I'll show you the murals."

"You've got a deal. Talk to you later." He closed the door and smiled as she drove away. He smiled all the way into the house as he headed toward the shower.

# CHAPTER NINE

"Everything looks wonderful," Cali said, later that morning as she looked at the decorations for the wedding. "Just beautiful."

"It'll look better when it's not set up in a storage area." Shar looked around the room with a critical eye. She wanted this wedding to be wonderful for Cali and Grant. And setting everything up here so that they could get a small sense of how it was actually going to come together out on the beach had been her idea.

Not only did it need to be picture-perfect for Cali, they were using the wedding in some advertisements on social media and in brochures. Because there was a lot of interest in Grant Ellington, the famous sea life artist and his wedding, Shar and Jillian had talked Cali into letting the resort gain some of that free publicity. But it had to be perfect.

Shar studied the white and soft blues that matched the water perfectly and the ribbons and lace, satisfied that this was going to be an outstanding wedding for her sister. The idea tugged hard at her heart in an unexpected moment of wistfulness.

"Put the water and the Lookout Point in the backdrop and it will be spectacular," she said.

"The wedding of the year." Jillian wiped tears from her eyes. "I am so overwhelmed. I'm speechless so I can't imagine how I'll be on the actual wedding day. Oh, Cali, this is what you deserve and this time you're going to get all your dreams."

Cali wiped tears from her own eyes and Shar had to fight not to start blubbering herself. Her heart wasn't quite as emotionally swayed as her sisters' but she would be an ice queen not to feel overwhelmed by the moment. "Y'all are going to have me blubbering soon." She laughed and wiped the dampness from her eyes.

Cali sniffed and put her arms around both of them. "Thank you both so much. My heart is so full of love. And though I never believed I'd marry again, now I can't wait. I keep saying that but it's just true."

"Keep saying it," Shar encouraged. "We're all in on your happiness, big sister." That made Cali smile. Shar, Jillian, and Olivia were triplets, so they'd all idolized Cali growing up. She was their quieter sister who'd ended up having a rough first marriage and they were just so glad to see her getting the happiness she deserved.

"Now if Olivia will just get here in time to spend some time with us, it will be perfect," Cali said.

"She'll be here," Jillian assured her. "I just talked to her."

"Great. Then we're all set." Cali took a deep breath. "Pinch me, please. Just so I know this is real."

Shar reached out and lightly pinched her elbow. "There you go. It's real all right."

"I guess we better get back to work then," Cali

said.

"Please, no. Mrs. Talbert Albert...I mean, Mrs. Albert Talbert's group arrives today."

And on that note, they left the storage area chuckling.

Shar was glad they found it funny because she didn't. She wanted to run into the ocean and swim for Key West.

By eleven, Gage headed to the resort. She told him to stop by and he wasn't a man who missed out on opportunity.

He felt as if he had come to know Shar in the last twenty-four hours. He'd been drawn to her on their first meeting but now he understood that her passion and her desire to make something better was part of the undeniable draw he felt toward her. That passion had nothing to do with dollars and cents or in taking over a business that had problems. It was simply about making something in the world better. Saving something beautiful so other generations could enjoy it. And that made the world better.

The resort was busy as he entered through the front doors. People and suitcases were everywhere. He assumed it had much to do with the tour bus sitting in the parking lot.

There were lines at the counter, so he decided that wasn't the way to go.

He spotted a young woman wearing a teal-toned Windswept Bay T-shirt and made his way through the throng to where she stood, directing people toward the elevators at the back of the lobby.

She was bright-eyed and young, maybe nineteen or a young-looking twentyish. "Can I help you?" she asked before he'd reached her.

He smiled. "I hope so. I'm looking for Shar. Do you happen to know where I can find her? She's expecting me."

"Sure, I can help you with that. See those stairs?" She pointed to the curving stairs in the corner. "If you follow them up to the next level and then walk down to those doors right there at the end, she's probably in there."

"Thank you." He paused. "What's going on, anyway?"

Her eyes widened. "Oh, this? There's a Georgia women's group here for the week. They are having a big conference and they booked the event to see the murals Grant Ellington painted and they hope to glimpse him while they are here during the wedding event."

"That's actually why I'm here. Shar promised to take me on a tour to view them."

The girl smiled. "You will love them. My boyfriend Jax helped paint them. Grant—I mean, Mr. Ellington—he was wonderful and generous. He saw a painting that Jax did at the Lagoon Adventures that he owns, and he asked Jax to assist him. Isn't that cool? Jax had never even thought about painting professionally until Mr. Ellington encouraged his talent. Now he is going to travel some with Grant." She blushed. "I mean, Mr. Ellington, and continue learning from him." She looked slightly flustered.

Gage gave her a pat on the shoulder, understanding her excitement. "It's a great opportunity. Jax must show some real talent."

"He does."

"I met Jax. He helped me replace a tire when I first came to town."

"Oh, he told me about that. Said he helped a nice guy out earlier this week. I'm Blair, by the way."

"I'm Gage Lancaster; it's nice to meet you."

"Likewise. You should go by the Lagoon. Jax said he hoped you would because he thought you really needed to have a little fun on this vacation." As soon as the words were out, she turned bright pink. "Oh, I mean, well, everyone has fun kayaking the lagoon."

Gage laughed. He liked the kid. "I'll do that. Jax was great. I'd like to check out his place and the painting that started all this."

He'd liked the younger guy who'd helped change his tire, when to be honest, Gage didn't have a clue what he was doing. Things like that drove him a little crazy. Every man should know how to change a flat, except he'd never had a need to learn. But he did not like feeling inadequate and that was exactly how he'd felt sitting on the side of the road with a flat.

"I'm going to go by there tomorrow and I'm going to take him up on that offer because you know what, Blair? Jax is absolutely right. I need to have some fun."

He thought of the day before and this morning, and knew it might just be hard to get him to leave when the time came.

From her vantage point in the office, Shar peeked through the crack between the door and the frame and eyed the group of ladies in the lobby. When Gage walked inside, her first inclination had been to hotfoot it down those stairs and throw herself at the man. But of course that was a no-no on so many levels that she dismissed the idea immediately. The other problem with it was there was no way she was going down those stairs to greet him while the *Magnolia Women* were checking into the resort.

Cali chuckled from behind her. "Go down there and meet Mrs. Albert Talbert."

Shar groaned. The woman had to have a name

other than her husband's name. But she had insisted several times Albert Talbert was what she wanted on her name tags and her room. And thus she was addressed that way. Why the man's parents had placed those two names together was mind-boggling. She could only imagine the teasing he must have endured with a name like that.

"You go down there. I have no desire to meet her firsthand. Over the phone was enough for me."

Jillian snorted, in a very uncharacteristic way. "I don't blame you. But you know you're going to have to deal with them, Shar. Cali has a wedding to get ready for."

She looked over her shoulder and glared at her sisters. "Excuse me, but that's why we hired Gracie. To handle these sort of situations."

"You're absolutely right," Cali said. "We still have to be involved, though."

She turned back and peeked again. Butterflies erupted in her chest as Gage started up the stairs. *What would her sisters think when they saw him?*

They might see right through her emotions and see

the attraction she had toward Gage. And that would not be good because she didn't want any encouragement. He would be leaving soon; she didn't know when but she knew that he would leave. He had a lot of responsibility on his shoulders and she'd already figured out that though he was taking time off, he wasn't a man to shortchange responsibility. *He would leave.* And she had to keep remembering that. It was the only way she could protect the feelings he evoked inside her.

She was going to have to dig deep not to let them see how he affected her. Because the man definitely affected her. She jumped back from the crack of the door as he reached the landing and headed toward the office.

"What's wrong with you?" Jillian asked. "You look like you've seen a ghost."

"No, no ghost." She was already not doing a very good job of covering up what she was feeling. The way he made her feel was one thing but then the fact that he was so interested in her work…he'd asked so many questions about everything that had to do with the turtles and that thrilled her. He got it, got her life's work and that was a hard thing to ignore.

A knock sounded on the door and startled her out of her daydreaming. She spun toward her sisters as their gazes riveted to the man in the open doorway. She stood behind the door where she'd had her eyeball glued to the crack and now she took a step out into the open so Gage could see her.

"Gage." She hoped she sounded surprised to see him.

"Hi." His gaze practically sopped her up. "You told me to stop by and you'd give me a tour." His eyes twinkled.

"Yes, I did. And now's the perfect time because…because I need to get out of the office and out of the building." She grabbed his arm and started to lead him toward the door on the opposite side of the room. It led out of the building.

"Hi," Cali interrupted her, coming from around her desk to meet Gage.

Jillian came to stand beside Cali and both of them looked at Gage with expectant expressions. "I'm

Jillian." She held out her hand. "I don't believe we've met."

"And I'm Cali and I *know* we haven't met."

Both her sisters shot her looks that said she'd clearly been keeping something from them.

"I'm Gage Lancaster and I feel like I've introduced myself a thousand times lately." His smile broadened into that time-stopping smile that he had and Shar felt it from head to toe. "I'm staying at a beach house down the beach from Shar. It's nice to meet the two of you."

"Likewise, I'm sure," Cali said.

Shar could hear the teasing in her voice as Gage shook her hand and then Jillian's.

Cali's expression brightened. "You helped Shar save the sea turtle."

"I did. But I wasn't much help; she had it all under control. She was amazing."

Shar felt her neck start to itch and warmth flowed through her at his words. And she didn't miss the look that passed between her sisters. That made her neck itch more.

When she met Gage's warm gaze, she broke out in goose bumps the size of eagle eggs.

Thankfully he broke the connection almost instantly as he shifted his attention back to Cali. "I understand congratulations are in order. I hear you and Grant Ellington are getting married this weekend."

"We are. Please, come join us. We'd love to have you. Since you're new on the island, you should come—shouldn't he, Shar? There will be a banquet and a dance under the moonlight afterwards. You need to come. We'd love to have you."

"Thank you. Shar has said the same thing."

"Oh really?" Cali asked, unmistakable delight in her voice. "That's good. Come."

Shar took his arm, feeling suddenly a little desperate to get out of the office. "I'm taking Gage to see Grant's murals by the pool and the beach. So, if anyone comes asking for me, you two feel free to handle whatever it is."

She started toward the door leading to the outside staircase and to her relief he didn't ask questions or try to stall. She opened the door and led the way out into the sunlight. She ignored the chuckles as the door closed behind them.

"Your sisters are nice. Friendly. You seem a little on edge."

She felt her brow crinkle in consternation. "A little. For one, they're tacking far too much onto me showing you around. And for two, they know I'm using you to avoid meeting Mrs. Albert Talbert."

"Oh, the infamous Magnolia Women's group is hers?" He teased.

"Yes." Shar made it down to the ground and stuffed her hands on her hips. "I left for the good of the resort. If I see the lady, she might 'oh honey' me or 'bless your heart' me, and I might lose it. I might mess up the whole good PR we're trying to get. Cali's the good one at that. I only agreed to try to help because she's got her wedding and then her honeymoon. I had to try. But ooh, I'm so not good at public relations."

"I'm sure it's not as bad as you say."

"Oh. It's bad—believe me. I'm trying to save the resort from losing money and its reputation right now."

She saw humor written all over his face. "Hey,

don't laugh. I do better with sea turtles and wildlife than being out there taking care of that kind of PR. If it wasn't for Cali getting married, that would not be my job description. I'd be outside. I'm more of a behind-the-scenes girl. Cali and Jillian take care of the other stuff." They'd reached the small bridge over the flamingo and swan lagoon that weaved its way through the resort. She started over it.

Gage's hand grasping hers, halting her. "I happen to think you're pretty terrific." He drew her into his arms.

She sucked in a breath, finding herself in his arms. "The mural is right over there—" Her knees nearly buckled as she looked up at him.

His lips hitched up at the corners. "I can't help myself," was all he said and then he lowered his head and kissed her.

# CHAPTER TEN

It was a slow kiss that curled Shar's toes and had her mind going all fuzzy.

Her hands reacted by going around his shoulders so she could hang on to him as her knees melted out from beneath her. And they did. Her entire body turned to liquid as the kiss went on.

"Well, hey there, sis."

At the unmistakable sound of her brother Jake's voice, Shar broke apart from Gage and found Jake grinning at her. She tried to look as if she were in control. She was not.

"Hey," she managed. Jake was a dive instructor and owned a diving shop in town. Feeling as if she might break out in hives, Shar met his curious gaze head on. "What are you doing here?"

His eyes crinkled at the edges with the want to smile. "I'm obviously not doing what you're doing."

To her relief, Gage introduced himself and shot her a wink. "You must be one of Shar's many brothers."

"Jake. I'm thinking I should be asking for your credentials and stuff because you know it's not every day that I find a man all snuggled up to my little sister."

Shar cut him with a glare. "Excuse me, I can kiss whomever I want, wherever I want."

Jake chuckled. "Obviously. I'm just startled finding you in a public place, all smoked up with a guy."

She glowered at him. "Cut it out, Jake." She turned to Gage to find him clearly enjoying the teasing that was going on. "Hey, you started this. My brother, one of the five, but maybe the nosiest of them all, wouldn't be gaping at me like that if you hadn't been kissing me."

"I don't care who sees me kiss you," Gage said.

Jake interjected, "You are in a public place. I'm not nosey, just observant."

She ignored Jake and also ignored Gage's statement, although she had to admit that she liked that he didn't care who saw them kissing. "Jake owns a dive shop and I guess most of his business stays under water, so he has no one to talk to until he comes and puts his nose into my business. What are you doing here anyway?" she asked.

"I had an errand to run."

She saw mischief written all over his face. "What kind of errand?"

"Nothing in particular. Just checking on the wedding plans."

"Uh-huh. No funny business," she warned. "You and your brothers better not be planning anything that will embarrass Grant or Cali. Or hurt the reputation of the resort. This is important."

He held up his hands. "I cannot believe that you

would even think that I—that we—would do something to harm the wedding."

She didn't believe him. "You're up to something. Do not think I don't recognize that twinkle in your eye. Heaven knows I was the recipient of the mischief behind that look many times growing up. I will personally hurt you if you goof this wedding up."

"Relax." He turned serious. "I would not mess this up for anything. I'm just having a good time yanking your chain." He grinned broadly.

And she saw Gage grin too.

"That being said, I'm still curious about why you're standing on the little white bridge all hugged up and kissing Gage."

"Go away," she demanded, struggling not to smile at the irritating brother who'd once tied her pigtails together while she slept.

"I'm going." He held out his hand to Gage. "Glad to meet you, man. Good to know someone can shake my tough sister up a bit with a little romance."

"Go," she ordered before Gage could say anything.

"Later, man," Jake said. "I better go now so I can live to dive another day."

Shar did not blush but she did get hot and she felt fumes heating up her cheeks. *Jake just went into the file with Meeks the plumber.* When she got the nerve to look at Gage, he was leaning against the bridge railing, arms crossed and smiling.

"He was just teasing you. No harm done."

"Easy for you to say. Now you know that having a big family does come with its drawbacks."

"I think you're just embarrassed and that's my fault. I'm sorry. And so you're the tough sister?"

She sighed, closed her eyes and counted to three as she fought to let the moment go. *Why had Jake's teasing gotten to her the way it had?* "I'm blunt. People take that as tough."

"You're also a kind-hearted softie."

That made her smile. "Well, don't tell anyone or it might ruin my tough gal reputation."

He pretended to seal his lips. "Done. Let's go see those murals."

She started to walk off the bridge; he fell into step

beside her and slipped his hand into hers. The simple, easy gesture caused butterflies to flutter in her chest. And Shar realized that she very much liked the feeling.

The pool and the mural came into view just a few steps from the bridge. "There it is." Shar halted and let him take in the full effect of the water scene in front of them.

"The main focus is sea turtles." He knew this had to mean a lot to Shar and the way she beamed as she looked at it told him he was right.

"McDreamboat did this to help bring attention to the sea turtles. And I love him dearly for it."

"It's fantastic."

"Takes your breath away, it looks so real."

"Definitely," he murmured, studying every aspect of it. Then he looked at her. *She* took his breath away. "There's a lot to take in on the giant wall."

"I know. And there are things hidden, like a small crab peeking out from behind a shell and things like that. We have a game card that kids—or adults, for that matter—can get at the towel cabana and the kids can mark off each listed hidden surprise as they find it. Everyone is loving it. That was Cali's idea because she knew that Grant liked to hide things in his paintings, so she made it into a game."

It was a brilliant idea, he thought. "I can't get over it. So Grant painted this and Jax helped?"

"Yes. Grant painted the majority of it, but Jax painted some of the plant life and the dolphin and other small creatures while McDreamboat, Grant"—she laughed—"focused on the focal points like the turtles. They did the same thing on the outside wall too. So do you know Jax?"

"I met him. I broke down on the side of the road the first morning I was heading into Windswept Bay. I have to admit that I've never had any reason to change a flat tire. I have a driver in the city and when I travel, I usually have drivers. Needless to say, I was in a predicament when Jax pulled in behind my car and took one look at me and knew I had no clue. He's a nice guy. I met his girlfriend Blair in the lobby."

"They're in love. And Jax is a good guy. I'm glad

he stopped to help you."

"Believe me, I needed it."

"Oh, I bet you would have figured it out one way or the other."

"Thanks for the vote of confidence."

She laughed again. "You're welcome. Stay out of Manhattan high-rises for a while and you'll be a regular person in no time."

"At the moment, I'm not even thinking about them." And he wasn't. He was thinking about getting her back in his arms and stealing another kiss. He shouldn't have kissed her earlier but he found himself acting on impulse when he was with her. And he wasn't going to feel bad about it because he'd do it again in a heartbeat.

"Let's head to the beach so you can see the masterpiece, the crowning jewel of the resort." She grinned. "It really is gorgeous. We are very lucky to have it. McDreamboat, and I do hope you know I call him that fondly, outdid himself on the exterior mural."

"So why do you call him McDreamboat?"

She chuckled. "Because he's got that Patrick

Dempsey look going…you do know about Dr. McDreamy from the TV series *Grey's Anatomy*?"

"Yes. I'd have to have been in a complete bubble if I didn't know about the show. I overheard the office secretaries talking about him and the show every Friday morning around the water coolers."

"Thought so. And don't feel left out, because you have the Paul Newman look going."

He laughed. "So you watch a lot of television?"

"Movies mostly. I love a great movie. *Cool Hand Luke* and basically any movie Paul Newman was in is a favorite. And I will admit that I, like most females across the country, tuned in at least a few times to get their McDreamy fix."

He shot her a skeptical look. "Paul Newman."

"You know—you have that square chin and those amazing baby-blue eyes."

He grinned. "So my eyes are amazing?"

"Are you fishing for more of a compliment? You know good and well you've got amazing eyes, among other extraordinary features."

"I'm not concerned about what I do or don't have

or what anyone else other than you thinks about my looks. But if you like something about me then I'm glad. I'll take whatever advantage I can get."

He reached for her and she slipped out of his grasp, laughing as she moved out ahead of him on the sandy path. "Oh no you don't. I'm not walking around a corner and having one of my other brothers pay me a surprise visit."

He grinned. "I don't mind."

"Well, I do."

He was laughing when she spun and looked up. He did the same and was instantly in awe. "Wow."

"Yeah, that's pretty much what everyone says. It's kind of amazing, isn't it?"

Gage studied the painting for a while. There was so much about it. Dolphins were the focal point here and a colorful coral reef. It was four stories high, facing the ocean.

"That's going to be a spectacular backdrop for the wedding. Didn't you say it was on the beach?"

"Yes, there." She pointed to an area. Behind it in the background was a cliff area with a lighthouse on it;

to the side was the ocean and then to the other side was the mural. And then behind them was the expansive beach and the line of resorts dotting the coastline. "Every aspect will be photo ready now."

"If I show up, will you dance with me?"

She turned to him and the ocean breeze had her dark hair dancing softly about her face. "Only if you behave."

"Now, where's the fun in that?"

"I'm serious, Gage. I need you to know I'm not an island fling. But I don't have my sights set on wedding bands either. So that puts this thing that's going on between us in a hard spot. You should know that."

He stepped toward her. "I'd never think you were a fling of any sort. I'm just asking if I show up, are you going to dance with me?"

She stared up at him with challenge in her eyes and after a moment, she nodded.

His pulse hummed as he wrapped one arm around her and drew her against him. "This is not a fling," he said, his voice rough, and then he kissed her again. Every ounce of him ached with the need to be closer to her. She moved in his arms. Her heart thundered against his as she gave in to the kiss; when her arms slowly came around him, the tension in him eased. He hadn't come here planning on this but he couldn't help himself. After far too short a moment, he made himself break the kiss and buried his face in her hair. The scent of sea breeze and some sweet scent filled his senses. "When I'm holding you, I feel like I've never felt before."

"Gage."

"Don't let that scare you off, Shar. I'm just telling you that's how I feel."

He leaned back and cupped her face, staring into her wide eyes. "Don't overthink this." He kissed the tip of her nose and then let her go. "Okay?"

"Okay," she said at last. "But I'm warning you like I warned my brothers: no acting up at the wedding. And that goes for the kissing thing too."

He grinned. "You know you enjoy the kissing as much as I do. I'll see you at the wedding."

# CHAPTER ELEVEN

"You look beautiful, Shar. I knew that color was going to bring out your eyes."

Shar heaved in a deep breath as she glanced at Cali and then stared down at the fairy-tale dress she wore. It was a soft sea-green sheath beneath an overlaying, swirling, flowing dress in a translucent sea-green. The skirt danced just above her knees and shimmered in the light with each move she made. The first time she'd tried it on at the bridal shop she'd thought it was gorgeous but now, her thoughts had taken on an altogether different tone. She wondered whether Gage would think she was beautiful in it.

She had not been able to get him and his tantalizing kisses off her mind during the last two days since she'd been in his arms on the beach.

"I think," she said slowly, "that is, other than your wedding dress, this is the most beautiful dress I've ever seen. And it's a bridesmaid dress. I was afraid as you and the rest of the family began to marry that I'd be like the woman in that movie *Twenty-Seven Dresses* and have a closet full of really ugly bridesmaid dresses."

Jillian chuckled from where she was pulling on her dress. "I had the same thought. With as big as our family is, and if our brothers' future fiancées ask us to be in their weddings, that the closet full of ugly dresses could be me."

"I would not put my sisters in ugly dresses." Cali looked indignant at the very thought.

Shar turned to give Jillian an are-you-kidding-me stare. "You'll all get married before me. I'm not even thinking I'm going to get married. I'm having too much fun being my own boss and doing what I love."

Cali turned to stare at herself in the mirror and ran a hand over her gorgeous dress. "Oh, you may change your mind when the man of your dreams walks into your life."

The dreamy tone of her voice rang an alarm bell inside Shar as Gage filled her thoughts. Since he'd come out of the surf toward her that first morning, her life had been in a tailspin. She couldn't deny it to herself...she wouldn't admit it to anyone else but it was true. Suddenly in her mind's eye, she saw him walking toward her, in black tuxedo pants and a crisp white shirt opened at the neck. And she was in a gorgeous wedding dress, holding a bouquet. She almost gasped the image was so real. So perfect.

*What was she thinking?* She gave herself a mental shake. She wasn't planning to get married. She wasn't. And for crying out loud, she hadn't even known him for a full week.

*It doesn't matter.*

It did matter. It mattered to her.

She focused on Cali. "This isn't about anyone but you today, Cali. And you look stunning."

"Oh, so true," Jillian added, coming to flank Cali as all three of them stared into the full-length mirror.

Cali smiled and then looked sad. "I just wish Olivia had made it."

Shar was ready to have a long conversation with her sister Olivia. She was being secretive and hadn't been home in months. And though she'd assured them that she wouldn't miss the wedding for anything, she was doing just that. She'd called Cali at the last minute and told her she couldn't make it. She hadn't even given any real reason other than the fact that she was very tied up in her project at the studio and she couldn't leave.

Shar was not happy about it. She wouldn't tell her sisters but she was starting to get a little worried. Olivia was acting…odd. This was unlike her. And that was a red flag to Shar.

To Cali, she only said, "I'm sure if she could have, she would be here. You know Olivia. She might have her sights set on those big dreams of hers but family is very dear to her heart. You are very dear to her."

And it was true. And that had Shar worrying all

the more.

The door opened and their mother walked in. Violet Sinclair was gorgeous, even at sixty. With her thick charcoal-gray hair and dancer's frame, she still carried herself like the dancer she'd been when she'd met and quickly married Sam Sinclair. She often told the story of how their dad had swept her off her feet when she'd come to the island for a couple of weeks of rest from a long dance tour. She'd been an independent, talented woman and she'd walked away from it and immediately began her large family.

Shar often wondered what her mother had done with those dreams she'd had before she married. Though there was nothing about her life that gave Shar reason to wonder. Violet was a nurturer who dove into raising and nurturing her family and the guests at the resort at the same time. To Shar, she was Superwoman but she could not stop wondering about her life before family.

"Mom," Cali gushed, spinning from the mirror and crossing to their mother with open arms. "What do you think?"

Violet's entire face lit with joy. "That you are gorgeous. But more important, I think you are going to be as happy and blessed in this marriage as I've been in mine."

*So much for Shar's questions.*

"I truly believe I will be. I wouldn't have said yes had I not thought so."

"Then, let's get this wedding started. I came for my hug and kiss and to let you know your father is ready, the family is gathered, but most important, your groom is anxiously waiting for his bride."

Cali teared up and so did Shar and Jillian. "Mom, so sweet," Cali managed through sniffles.

Shar dabbed at her eyes. "Mom, yes, sweet, but we had all this makeup put on and now you're going to ruin it with one beautiful line."

That made everyone laugh and helped ease the touching moment.

Smiling, Violet cupped Cali's cheek. "Give me five minutes to get out there to my seat and the wedding planner can get this wedding started."

And then she left and Cali's hand went to her

stomach. "I keep hearing Elvis singing that song 'I'm So Happy I Could Die.' Or toss my cookies."

And with that, they all burst into giggles.

The music played as Shar walked down the carpeted path to stand beside Jillian. Because she could not choose between her sisters, Cali had them both acting as maids of honor; Shar carried the ring and would pass it to Jillian, who would pass it to Cali. The music switched, signaling Cali was about to start her walk down the small aisle.

Shar found herself watching Grant as he watched Cali walking toward him. The expression of love on his face, in his gaze said that this was their moment. Love was written all over his face.

He would be good to her sister and after all that Cali had gone through in her first marriage, she deserved nothing but happiness. Shar loved Grant for his love of her sister and she knew in her heart of hearts that this was the beginning of their happily-ever-after.

Her thoughts shifted to Gage and Shar focused on the wedding, not on the unexplainable, overpowering emotions just the thought of him caused in her.

"I now pronounce you husband and wife. What God has joined together, let no man tear apart." The words of the preacher startled Shar out of her wandering thoughts. Somehow she'd handed the ring over when she was supposed to but she'd been thinking about Gage.

*What was wrong with her?*

She focused on Cali and her McDreamboat of a brother-in-law as Grant took Cali in his arms and kissed her. Shar found herself looking out across the audience toward the reception area and there, standing near the side of the building, she caught a glimpse of Gage. Instantly she felt weak with seeing him. Her stomach dipped as she met his intense gaze.

And in that moment, nothing else mattered.

Something about this place had Gage's senses in hyper drive. *Or was it just Shar?* Not just Shar but Shar in all her alluring ways. He was realizing that it didn't matter whether she was saving a sea turtle, a puppy, or just looking at him with those eyes of hers: she got to him. And watching her as she moved forward, following the happy couple off the small platform where the wedding had been conducted, he knew she was his destiny.

He had purposefully stayed away from her the last two days, giving her time to take care of the wedding plans and enjoy her family. But it was also to give himself time to cool down, back up, and try to get his head on straight.

He'd arrived early, unable to stop himself from watching her in the wedding. He wanted to see Shar in the wedding. He'd been standing at the edge of the building, virtually invisible with the crowd that was gathered around watching from afar, and yet she'd looked out over the crowd and her gaze had found his. Now, as she reached the reception area, she glanced his way; he winked at her and saw the smile light her eyes. She was swept into a round of photos with the family and it was much later when she finally made her way through the crowd to him.

He kept his hands to himself, though he wanted nothing more than to pull her into his arms. "You're beautiful and stunning this evening."

"Thank you. I tried to clean up as good as I could."

He chuckled and shot her an approving head-to-toe look. "You did a great job."

"Cali picked out the dress. Come on, I'll introduce you to Grant and the rest of my family."

Her brothers all stood in a group, looking more than ready to peel off their jackets but a photographer buzzed around them, having them do different poses. Like he'd feel, they looked as if they were about at the end of their posing ropes.

"Are some of your brothers twins?" There was no mistaking that Jake and one of the brothers looked a lot alike. Though Jake had longer hair and the other brother wore a five-o'clock shadow. And the two together looked nothing like the other three brothers. And those three brothers looked strikingly alike but one looked slightly older.

"You're right. Cam's the oldest, then Levi and Trent are twins. And then Jake and Max look a lot alike but are a year apart. Their parents were killed in an accident and my parents adopted them. They grew up with us and my parents were already their godparents so they are my brothers from another mother and pop."

"So, a set of twins and triplets in one family."

"Bingo, you get a gold star." She smiled and then tapped the female photographer on the shoulder. "I think they've had enough. Can you grab some promo shots from the other aspects of the wedding?"

The woman glanced back at the five men and smiled. "I can, but believe me, your brothers are going to make some stunning shots..." She paused as she focused on Gage. "You're Benjamin Lancaster." She stepped back and aimed her camera. "More good promo of the rich and famous at the resort. Smile, you two."

Shar glanced at him and he smiled. "Promo for your resort," he said and she smiled up at him. Just as the flash went off.

"Great," the photographer said. "How about I get one with you and the brothers? And if I could get Grant over here, it would be an amazing shot. Might even make a cover shot. I'll be right back."

Shar glared after the woman. "I tell you, the publicist hired her and she's one pushy lady."

"But she'll have you some good promo shots for the resort when she's done. I've learned in this life that sometimes if you're not pushy you don't get what you want. If you want something or have a job to do, either way you've got to go for it."

"Well, if you put it that way, then she is going to go far."

He smiled. "Works for me."

"Gage." Jake stepped up. "You still hanging around my sister?" He grinned at Shar.

"I am. How are you?"

"I'm good. Be better when I can peel this monkey suit off but all in all, doing well. Come on, I'll introduce you to the brothers. Don't you need to go

133

tend to some photo ops, sis? Looks like the warriorgrapher—the photographer—is gathering up the ladies now."

"Ugh." Shar sighed when she saw Jake was right. "I'll be back."

She hurried off and Gage watched her weave through the crowd.

"You know, she doesn't date much. How are you managing being around?"

"Luck, I guess."

Jake laughed. "Maybe."

One of the brothers—looked like maybe the oldest of the group, maybe thirty-five—held his hand out. "I'm Cam. The older brother of this baseball team. You've obviously got something going for you. This is Levi, chief of police, so remember he's got his eye on you. This is Max, Trent, and you know Jake."

Each man held out his hand and shook. Gage felt as if he were under a microscope as they all stared at him with open curiosity.

"What brings you to the island?" Levi asked.

Jake nudged his brother. "Okay, Chief, don't go all detective on him. We don't want to run him off. From the way Shar's been acting lately, she might come after you for doing it."

All the brothers studied him and he realized that Jake had filled them in on the kissing on the bridge incident.

"He won't run me off. And it's fine. I'm here for some time off."

"It's a good place for that," Max said. "You should do some diving while you're here. Jake's is the place to go."

"I've never dived."

"You're missing out, man." Jake tapped his chest. "Come see me and I'll fix you up."

"I might do that."

"You won't be sorry. Better yet, get Shar to bring you over."

He hadn't known how the brothers would react to him, especially once he realized Jake had told them about finding him kissing Shar. But he quickly figured out that they were protective of her and concerned for her but happy she was seeing someone.

That being said, he knew without thinking too hard about it that none of them would like it if she were hurt.

Which he had no plans to do.

# CHAPTER TWELVE

Shar headed back to rescue Gage from her brothers when a short, plump, pretty woman cut her off. She had intensely white hair styled to perfection and bright rose lipstick.

"Shar Sinclair," she drawled in a thick Southern way.

Instantly Shar's spirits sank. She'd managed to hide out all week from the nightmare that was Mrs. Albert Talbert.

"It's me, Mrs. Albert Talbert."

As if Shar needed clarification.

"I've been looking for you all week. Bless your heart, you must not work but a few hours of the day."

Shar forced a smile. "Mrs. Talbert." The words came out stiff. "I hope you are enjoying your stay." She'd heard the woman was looking for her and she'd made certain to not be around at those times. It had made her feel a little bad but she really hadn't tried too hard.

"That's why I've been hoping to see you. We have had an absolutely wonderful time. Wonderful, I tell you. You may have had a rough time getting all the details right, forcing me to stay on your case much more than I would normally have to do but..." She paused dramatically. "In the end, you and your resort have come through with flying colors. I'm making the recommendation to the committee that we have a ladies' retreat here at least once a year."

Shar could not believe her luck. "That's wonderful to hear. I'm thrilled you and all the ladies had such a good time."

"You must give that Gracie a raise. That young woman gets every detail right and I not once had to tell her she'd gotten some detail wrong."

Shar gritted her teeth. "Isn't that wonderful." She felt someone at her elbow. *Gage.* Her mouth went dry as he smiled at her and then held his hand out.

"I'm Gage Lancaster."

"Oh, and I'm Mrs. Albert Talbert." Her pink lips flashed instantly into a wide smile. "Hon, is this handsome man yours?"

Shar almost laughed and started to tell the woman no but Gage took her hand in his.

"Yes, ma'am, I am. And if you would excuse us, I've been promised a dance by the lovely Shar."

"Of course. I think I see Grant Ellington heading to the punch bowl. I need a photo with him. Thank you again, Shar. We leave early tomorrow but I'll see you next year."

"Not if I see you first," Shar said under her breath.

Gage laughed softly in her ear as he pulled her into his arms and spun them out onto the dance floor. "You're all tensed up. Relax," he coaxed, and his warm breath tickled her ear.

"Thanks for rescuing me." She looked at him.

"I couldn't help noticing from across the way that you looked stiffer than a steel poker, so I thought I'd see if I could help."

"I do like an observant man."

"Anything for the pretty lady. And just so you know, I am yours."

His soft words echoed through Shar; she faltered and stepped on his foot.

"Gage." She looked up at him. "What are you doing? You barely know me. You're going back to New York next week or soon after that—"

"Maybe not."

"Well, I'm not going there. I told you, I don't want—"

He pulled her closer against him. "You don't want what, Shar? Love, passion, desire? Because I feel that for you. All of it. And I do know you. You can't tell me you don't feel it. Because I know you do."

Shar moved automatically to the rhythm of the slow dance, but her mind was in chaos. She shook her head. "No, some people get swept off their feet. Not me. I have a life of my own, Gage."

His heart beat with hers, as if her heart and his heart were locked together in a dance, intricately intertwined together. She tried to pull away, tried to put distance between them but his arm held her gently but firmly with him.

All the thoughts of him, the daydreams rushed at her. *They were just daydreams. Not really what she wanted. Were they?*

She raised her gaze to him and he kissed her forehead. "I would never take you away from your beloved sea turtles. I see the value of your work and it is the first thing about you that I fell in love with."

The music faded. They were at the edge of the dance floor and Gage pulled her into the shadows. Shar fought what he was saying. Tried to understand why he would be saying these things so quickly. So suddenly. "Gage, you've suffered the death of your last living parent. You're overworked, torn and here to sort your life out. And to mourn. You are..." She searched for words. "You are putting emotions on me somehow. That's it. You need time to adjust to what's happening in your life. I'm just an escape from it. That's it. I'm an escape. The sea turtle rescue started it. Don't you see?"

He stared at her and said nothing.

"You know I'm right." She felt more certain that she'd hit exactly on his problem. And the feelings she'd so suddenly and quickly felt for him were because she was drawn to rescue living things.

"You really believe that?"

She nodded, as her head buzzed with thoughts and remembrances of his touch, his kisses, his laughter. "What you think you feel for me isn't real. You're…you're a ship trying to find your anchor."

He'd just been staring at her, his jaw tight. Behind him, the ocean glistened in the moonlight. Now his brows knit and his blue gaze flashed; she saw it even in the dim light.

"I know what I feel, Shar. You're right—I am a ship trying to find my anchor but that doesn't mean I don't have a clear head. I know what I want. And I want you."

She stepped back, panicked. "I…I warned you. I told you I wasn't looking for anything. I have my life. I need to get back to the wedding. They'll be cutting the cake and I need to be there for Cali. They'll be leaving soon."

The look in his eyes cut through her and she fought not to reach for him. "I'm sorry, Gage." Not waiting for him to say more, she spun and walked back to the wedding party. Her stomach churned like waves in an angry sea. But she put one foot in front of the other and walked on.

It was the only thing she could do right now.

Gage shoved a hand through his hair and watched Shar walk away from him. *What was wrong with him?* He suddenly felt like a number-one royal mess-up.

He could walk into a room and negotiate mega deals but where she was concerned, he couldn't even keep his head on straight. He'd pushed too fast, too hard. And this was what it got him. Standing under the moonlight—alone.

Feeling like a royal jerk, he strode back to the reception and headed toward the parking lot. Maybe Shar was right. Not about how he felt about her, because she was dead wrong about that. He'd fallen in love with her and nothing could change that. But where his dad was concerned and his life, maybe he had been focusing on her rather than getting everything else dealt with.

He slid into his car and slammed the door. Gunning the engine, he backed out of the parking lot. The tires squealed as he turned onto the road and sped toward his rental. Not even bothering to open the garage, he parked in the drive and stalked to the front door and let himself inside.

Stopping in the dark kitchen with only the moonlight shining through the expansive windows, he headed out to the deck. It would be a long time before he'd sleep—if he did at all.

Shar had warned him. She'd told him she wasn't on the market and he'd pushed her. He'd been the one who'd pursued her, kissed her. It had all been initiated by him and she'd warned him all along the way. Even when she hadn't verbalized it, he'd known it was there by the look in her eyes and different signs.

And still he'd pushed. Believed what he was seeing at other times and feeling in her responses to his kisses that she was feeling what he was feeling and just denying the strength of their connection.

*Had he been wrong about her feelings?*

*Or was she hiding from her feelings? Or maybe from something else?*

It was nearly three in the morning when, with no idea where to go next with Shar, he finally pushed up out of the chair, damp from the night fog that had rolled in. When he walked into the house, he realized that it was unusually dark. *Had it been this dark before?* With no moonlight streaming in, he noticed there was no blue light coming from the electric pads of the microwave or the stove. No lights of any kind anywhere.

The electricity was out.

Fishing his phone from his pocket, he clicked on the flashlight app and went back out into the garage in search of the breaker box. He found it in the storage room behind a stack of storage boxes. Setting his phone down, he pushed the stack of boxes out of the way. But when he went to open the breaker box, he hit the top box with his arm and it crashed to the floor. "Perfect," he muttered, studying the breaker box to see whether any of the main breakers had blown. *Nope.* He was going to have to call the electric company—the lights suddenly came on and flooded the room with light.

*Great, at least that was one problem he hadn't had to fix.*

He saw that the box had been filled with books. He bent to one knee and sat the box upright and then started putting books inside. He saw a photo had slipped from one of the books and was hanging halfway out. He went to push it back into the book and stopped...it was a picture of his dad. *What was his dad's picture doing in this house?*

# CHAPTER THIRTEEN

Shar held Rufus tightly in her arms and held her emotions in even tighter. She'd been numb ever since she'd walked away from Gage. She'd had to focus on Cali. It was Cali's night and nothing in her life could interfere with making sure her sister had the perfect wedding reception and was sent off on her honeymoon with hugs and kisses and a beautiful event.

That Shar was falling apart inside was of little importance. At least then. Now, staring out her window into the dark, murky night, she was a basket case and it was all Gage's fault. *Darn the man!*

She scratched Rufus's head and then buried her face in his scruffy neck. "Why, why, why, did I let myself get into this spot, Rufus?"

At the sound of his name, the pup barked.

She heaved a sigh and looked back up. It was nearly two and she had a busy day starting in about five hours. She had to at least try to get some sleep. And maybe things would look better in the daylight.

She'd just crawled into bed when the lights went out.

*Great. Just great.*

It was pitch black because the fog had set in earlier and covered up the moonlight. Rufus had been curled up at her feet. Now he moved up the covers and curled up against her chest.

"You're right, fella. I can't do anything about this right now either so here I shall stay, curled up with you."

Closing her eyes, she laid there. And laid there. She opened her eyes and stared up at the ceiling...or where the ceiling was supposed to be. She couldn't see it, so she stared up at the darkness...and thought of

Gage.

By the time sunrise broke the horizon, Gage had found more pictures of his dad and a woman he did not recognize. Shock and even anger had been his constant companion with each photo he found. And in some of the photos there was a boy, a toddler. And it wasn't him.

*Who were these people?*

*Why were they here in this house?* He had questions and he would have them answered in a few hours when he started making calls to his office and his dad's lawyers. That was the only place he knew to start looking for answers. Larry Stewart had been his father's friend and lawyer for years. If anyone knew who this was, it would be Larry. But another question he wanted answered was why did Kym send him here? There was no way this could be a coincidence. No way.

He stared at the photo album that lay open on the kitchen island. He'd been looking at this one for a while now. The woman was beautiful; she had blonde hair and she looked to be around her dad's age—maybe ten years younger. That would put her in her early fifties now, maybe even late forties. She might be younger than his dad but they looked happy. His dad looked happy.

There were pictures of them on a sailboat out in the bay. Pictures of them on the beach and his dad was smiling. His dad not only looked happy—he looked happier than Gage had ever seen him.

He looked at the time on his phone and thought about waking Kym or Larry up but instead he went to the bathroom and took a much-needed shower. His thoughts went to Shar as it always did at this time of morning.

*Where was she running today? What would she save today?*

He wanted to find her, to tell her he'd rushed her and that he'd slow down. But instead he would give her space. And he would deal with his own business. His new business: discovering who his dad was when he hadn't been in Manhattan.

His dad had died too young at fifty-nine. And he'd obviously had secrets.

Half an hour later, he walked downstairs, picked his phone up off the bar and strode out onto the deck and called Kym.

She answered at the first ring. "You called. At last," she gushed. "Benjamin, if you don't do something, the London deal is gone. They are breathing down our necks and I'm holding them off but I'm afraid if I don't tell them something soon—"

"I don't pay you to tell me what to do, Kym," he snapped, and then grimaced and sighed. "Look. I'll deal with it. But right now I want to know why I just found photos of my dad in this house you rented for me."

Silence.

"Because…look, if you would come home for the reading of the will… Mr. Stewart has been calling too. He left a message for you to get in touch with him ASAP."

"Why are the pictures here, Kym? You know something and I want it now." He was firmer than he'd ever been with her. He wasn't like that normally but this was not normal and she was obviously hiding something important from him.

"Because, it's your house."

Her words didn't come as much of a surprise. He'd gone over everything about the situation that he knew and this was no coincidence. "And why do you know this and I don't?"

"Because, once when Mrs. Davies was out sick, she had to have me take care of a rental booking. There had been some sort of problem and the rental company had a big mix-up and she couldn't handle it because she was sick. She said that there was to be no mention of the incident to anyone. Absolutely no one, including you."

"And why is that?" He didn't say anything about what was in the photos. Not until he suspected whether she knew about the people in them.

"I honestly don't know. I, well, when you needed a place to stay, to disappear, I remembered about the house and I thought it would be a good place. I...the house was used as a rental. I had no idea there were pictures there. If you come for the reading of the will, I'm sure you'll find out everything."

"I'll call Larry." He started to hang up and then stopped himself. "And I'll get back to you on when I'll deal with London. Let them know I'm setting up a date."

"I'll tell them. And, I'm sorry. I didn't mean—"

"It's fine. I've got to go."

He immediately called Larry.

The hospital was busy with tours and Shar intentionally tried to work out of the spotlight. Today she helped feed the turtles and then she helped Alex with the medicine.

John had a day off today and she was covering for him.

"So, I saw you dancing at the wedding last night with Gage. How's that going?"

She cut her eyes from the paper on the clipboard she was making notes on and his eyes widened. "That good? From the looks of it, I thought there was something going—"

"I really don't want to talk about this right now."

"Hey." He held his hands up in surrender. "I'm just making an observation."

"Well, don't."

They both went back to work, only her thoughts were instantly back on Gage. After a minute, she couldn't keep quiet. "Hard-headed man," she muttered.

"Me or can I take a wild guess and say Gage?"

"Yeah, Gage. The man, even though I told him I wasn't interested in getting serious with anyone, he goes and tries to tell me that he's serious. It's been what? All of seven days since I met him! You don't fall in love in seven days. You just don't." She tapped the pen on the clipboard and glared unseeing at the words there. After a few taps, she realized Alex hadn't said anything. She looked up to find him studying her with an odd expression. "Well, what?"

"You...are mad at the guy because he said he loved you?"

She jammed a fist to her hip. "Did you not hear the seven days part of what I just said?"

He looked indifferent. "Yeah, well, I guess if the guy feels it, he feels it."

She glared at him. That was not what she wanted to hear.

"Hey, look, Shar, don't look at me that way. I, for one, am your friend. But that doesn't dismiss the fact that I had to come to grips with the fact that that's all we will ever be. And that was because you said so."

"Don't go there, Alex. We are friends. I can't make it more than that. But you know I've always cared about you since we were in school. As a friend."

He looked frustrated but they'd been over this. She hadn't gone into the specifics that day that Gage had asked her about Alex because there was no need. *But now, seeing that Alex might still think—*

"Look, Shar. I get it. I understand it but, yeah, I have to say that when I saw the way Gage was looking at you the other night, I felt a jab in the gut. I can't help but still wish there was more between us. But that's just coming from my side. But you're different right now. You looked at him different. There was— well, to be frank, there was heat coming off the two of you that rivaled what was coming off Cali and Grant. You might be mad at the guy but you're lying to yourself if you say there's nothing there. And I don't care if it's seven days or two years. When something charges you up, it charges you up and until today the only thing I've seen have this much fire coming off you is saving a sea turtle."

Shar's mouth had dropped open and she snapped it shut as she considered what he'd said. "But—"

The scanner in the corner went off. Odell from the call room's voice crackled over the line. "Emergency call. Sea turtle in distress at the base of Lookout Point."

The base of Lookout Point was connected to the resort beach. She and Alex went in to motion at the same time and headed toward the ambulance.

Shar pushed her own troubles aside as she climbed into the passenger's seat and buckled in. Her adrenaline was pumping as Alex climbed behind the wheel and shot her a glance.

"You all right?"

She nodded. "I'm fine. Let's go save a turtle."

# CHAPTER FOURTEEN

Gage climbed out of his car and stared at the resort. His bag was tossed in the passenger seat and the private plane would be arriving at the airport within the hour. He'd tried to tell himself to just get on the plane, but he couldn't leave without at least telling Shar good bye.

He'd talked with Larry Stewart and could no longer put off going back. He had responsibilities and employees of the firm needed to know the company was going to be fine since the sudden death of his dad. And he had to handle the London deal. But first the will needed to be read and Larry had assured him there was information that would only be revealed during that time. He wasn't authorized to share anything with Gabe until then. Gage had hidden out long enough.

Still, he hadn't been able to drive by the resort without stopping. He hated to leave not just because of Shar but there were so many things he hadn't done here on the island that he'd wanted to do with her. He hadn't taken Jax up on his offer and gone by the Lagoon Adventures. He hadn't gone by and taken Jake up on snorkeling.

And he hadn't convinced Shar that he loved her.

He had left unfinished business in New York and he was leaving unfinished business here. It seemed like his new pattern. Only he had no plans to let anything go undone. He never had.

But at the moment New York waited.

And who knew, time away might be exactly what he and Shar needed.

He was halfway across the parking lot when he heard the siren. He recognized the sound and spun to see the Windswept Bay Sea Turtle Hospital ambulance roaring down the road. Gage's adrenaline kicked in and he took a step back toward his car. They might need help and he knew that where that ambulance was, Shar would be there too. He was reaching for the door handle of his car, expecting the ambulance to fly by the resort and he was going to have to act fast to catch it, or at least keep it in his sights. But, to his surprise, it slowed and then swerved into the resort drive and sped past him through the parking lot to a gate at the back of the property. Shar jumped from the passenger's seat, ran to the gate and swung it open. Gage ran to catch up to her and reached her just as the ambulance drove through the opening.

"Shar," he called, getting her attention. "What's up?"

Surprise lit her face when she saw him. "A sea turtle was found on the beach and it's in a really bad way. It was hit by a boat prop."

She was starting to close the gate and the ambulance was waiting on her. "Go." He took the gate. "I've got this."

She nodded and didn't wait for more as she jogged

to the open door of the ambulance and jumped inside. Immediately it started moving across the sand toward the beach. Gage closed the gate and ran to catch up. He had left his suit jacket in the car, but wore a crisp, white, hand-tailored shirt with his dress slacks and Italian loafers—none of which was about to appreciate the sand and surf. Didn't matter, Shar had been upset about the condition of the turtle and she might need him.

The ambulance was at the base of Lookout Point and he pushed through the crowd and saw Shar and Alex kneeling beside a huge turtle that was still in knee high water. It looked bad.

It had a huge chunk out of its shell revealing a terrible wound and there was also a huge gash in its head. The sight caused his stomach to lurch but he ignored it and moved forward.

"What can I do?" He jogged into the water.

Shar's hair was blowing in the wind and there was fire in her eyes like that first morning he saw her. There was a fierceness to her. *Dear heaven above, I love her with every fiber of my being.* God had made a warrior queen when he'd fashioned Shar and she was meeting her calling head on. His heart slammed against his chest as she glared up at him.

"We have to get him to shore."

"Help her. I'll get the wench ready." Alex let go of the turtle then paused. "Good to see you, Gage. We can use you." And then he jogged toward the ambulance.

Shar was holding onto the turtle and clearly it was not good. Up close it was even worse than he'd suspected. He grabbed the turtle and helped hold it.

Shar looked at him. "You're going to ruin your clothes," she snapped, "But thank you."

"They're clothes, Shar. This is a sea turtle and he needs us."

Her eyes flared and then she blinked hard and he knew she was fighting back tears. "He's in a really bad way. His spinal cord is exposed and...it's just not good," she managed.

He smiled at her across the turtle. "He's got you and Alex and the hospital to help him now. He'll make it."

She nodded and took a deep breath then cleared

her throat. She looked at the people on shore who were watching with concern written on their faces. "I need you three," she nodded toward a group of strong looking teenagers. "Can you give us a hand?"

And just like that the tears were gone and the warrior was back and taking control.

The muscled teens came forward immediately. From their swift reaction Gage figured they'd just been waiting to be told it was okay to help.

"What do you want us to do?"

Shar nodded toward the ambulance where Alex was pulling a carrier from inside. "My partner is bringing a carrier. We'll get it under him and then it'll take all of us to get him to the ambulance and onto the lift. He's a big one."

"We got this," one of them said and the others agreed.

Alex reached them. The carrier had strong poles with what appeared to be strong canvas attached to each.

"Take this." He handed Gage one side. "Like Shar said, we're going to get this under him and then we'll lift."

Shar lifted one hand off the turtle and pointed to the sides of the turtle. "Everyone take hold. Help hold him steady, and floating. Alex and Gage will get the carried under him."

Working together they managed to get the canvas under him and the poles on either side. It didn't take as long as Gage thought it would. The teens were great and he could read it in their expressions that they felt the undeniable adrenaline rush of knowing they were saving something magnificent. Just like he felt every time he had helped.

"Now grab onto the poles. On the count of three we're going to all lift and start toward shore." Shar grabbed the pole in the center. Gage took the head of the pole beside her and Alex took the other pole across from him as two guys took their places beside Alex and one took the end on the other side of Shar.

She counted to three and they all lifted. The turtle was dead weight and huge—Gage figured he had to be four hundred pounds. He was much larger than Don Juan.

When they finally had him loaded Shar climbed in with the turtle.

"You okay?" he asked Shar as he started to close the doors behind her.

"I'm good."

He wanted to say more but now wasn't the time. "Okay, good to know." He closed the doors.

Alex was addressing the teens. "Come by the hospital anytime and check on him. Are you guys the ones who called it in?"

"Yeah, we did."

The big blond guy shrugged. "He looked hurt so Chad remembered seeing the hospital sign and googled the hospital number."

Chad looked worried. "Is he going make it?"

"Hopefully. He's bad but y'all found him so he's got hope. We've got to go, but check on him at the hospital. We'll give you updates and we need a name. You guys get to name him."

They all brightened. Chad grinned. "We're Mustangs. That's our football team. And we never give up. State champs this year. Name him that."

"Yeah," one of the biggest guys chimed in. "Mustang."

"He'll make it," the blond added. "He won't give up. He made it to shore didn't he."

Alex grinned. "Mustang he is. Gotta go. Y'all did good."

Gage was already climbing into the passenger seat when Alex climbed behind the wheel. He shot Gage a grin and started the engine. "Hang on, Shar. We're moving out. And we've got a shotgun rider."

Gage looked into the rear and saw Shar look over her shoulder. Their gazes locked and she gave a nod. "Move it, Alex. I've got the IV started," was all she said as she turned back and went to work pulling bags of liquid from the shelves.

Gage didn't buckle up but waited so he could jump out and open the gate. When he climbed back inside Shar looked over her shoulder.

"Thanks for helping, Gage."

"I wouldn't miss this for the world. Let's roll, Alex."

Three hours later Shar walked out of the surgery

room. Tired but hopeful she pulled off her vinyl gloves and tossed them in the trash. There was so much to be grateful about. It was a miracle Mustang had made it to shore and that the football players had seen him floundering. Mustang was very lucky not to have died and washed up to shore.

And since surgeons didn't just stand around the hospital waiting for injured turtles to show up they'd lucked out that one had been at the Marathon Keys Hospital just finishing a scheduled surgery. Mustang didn't have time for a scheduled one. The surgeon had caught a helicopter and been here within the hour and now Mustang was holding his own.

Now, it was time to see Gage. After he'd assisted the team in getting Mustang inside he'd borrowed someone's phone and was out in the parking lot deep in conversation.

She and Alex had both scrubbed up to assist the surgeon in surgery since John was off. That had been three hours ago. Now, she looked around for Gage but didn't see him. She walked outside looking for him and that was when it hit her that he wasn't there. He'd left.

Her chest was tight with emotions as she walked back inside the building.

Odell stuck her head out of the dispatch room. "You lookin' for that hunk of charm and pizazz that was in here. If so, I've got a note for you."

"Why didn't you say so before?" Shar took the note out of Odell's outstretched hand.

"Thought you'd take it," the older woman said, grinning.

"Thanks." Shar said. "Did he leave?"

"Yep. Caught a taxi over an hour ago. Not that he looked too happy about it. Wrote you that note and asked me to give it to you soon as you were out of surgery."

Shar's stomach felt bottomless as she went back outside and tore the note open.

*Shar,*

*You made a difference today. You always do. Keep it up. I had to go. People are waiting and no way out of it today. Like you said, I have things I need to confront.*

*You were, and always will be, amazing. But then,*

*I've found that when I'm somewhere with you…amazing is just to be expected.*

*Gage*

Tears sprang to her eyes. He was gone.

She stood and looked as a sense of panic rose inside her. She'd messed up. Where was he?

*He'd been amazing.*

He'd come out of nowhere looking like he'd stepped out of a *GQ* magazine in a suit that was tailor made for him…and he'd raced into that water without a care in the world that he was ruining his clothes. He'd just wanted to help save a sea turtle.

From the first moment she'd met him he had a heart for the things that mattered to her. He'd connected with her on a level that no one ever had before. But so had she with him.

As much as she wanted to deny it she couldn't. Couldn't fight her love for him because she feared that somehow admitting she cared for him would change who she was because she knew now that argument wasn't going to work. She loved him.

She needed to see him. To…to talk…to tell him.

She just needed to see him.

She raced inside. "Odell. Where did he go?"

"Honey, I told you. He didn't tell me. But, I did hear him on the phone with someone and I'm pretty sure it was someone who was at the airport."

"Thanks. Tell Alex I had to run."

"I heard you."

She spun and Alex stood in the doorway. "Drive safe. And don't be a jerk. Give the guy a chance."

She laughed. "Tell me how you really feel."

"Don't be a jerk. Now go."

She was already fishing her keys out of her pocket as she headed for the exit.

He had at least an hour head start. It was a long shot but it was all she had and it...

It wasn't enough.

An hour later she stood in the airport and felt completely devastated that she didn't see him and at a loss how to find him if he was there.

The only thing she had to go on was that he'd sounded like he was going back to New York and all the flights to New York had already left. So there she stood. In the middle of the terminal wondering why she'd thought she could find him in an airport in the first place.

It wasn't as if this was a movie where she would catch him just before he went through security. It also, it appeared was not the movie that he suddenly decides not to get on his flight and run through the airport to her. No, this was real life and there were people everywhere. This was real life and things like that didn't happen.

At least not to her.

And now she had no clue what to do next.

She rubbed her cold arms and waited in the center of the ticket area just in case she was wrong and he was going to show up.

But no, no fairy tale. This was not a Hallmark movie.

But oh how she wished it was.

# CHAPTER FIFTEEN

Gage hadn't wanted to leave Florida. And after helping save the turtle he'd at least wanted to tell Shar goodbye. She might not want him in her life but he still wanted to tell her goodbye.

But in the end, while she was tied up in surgery there was no other way. So he left her a note. He had to make it to Stewart Law Offices that afternoon. Larry had pushed the meeting back from four to six o'clock so that Gage's plane could get him there from Florida. He'd landed and then immediately boarded a helicopter that carried him to a landing pad at the top of the building that housed the offices of both Stewart Law and Lancaster Industries.

He'd walked into Larry's office at five till six. And now, in utter shock he stared across the desk at the man who obviously knew his own father better than Gage had.

"Let me get this straight. You're telling me I have a younger brother?" Larry hadn't stumbled over his words. He'd spoken clearly and still Gage hadn't processed what he'd just heard Larry say as he read the will his father had left.

"You heard me correctly. As your dad stated, he had another child by Elizabeth Jackson. They were never married, though I can tell you it wasn't because your father didn't want to marry her. She refused. Your brother's name is Brandon Jackson and you were four when he was born."

Gage stood and paced the width of the room before he stopped to stare out the high rise window. They were twenty floors up; he had a view of the Empire State Building in the distance.

*I have a brother.*

The news began to sink in. He turned. "Where is he? What does he do? Why haven't I known this?" He had so many unanswered questions.

"Your dad had planned to tell you. He just died before he got the chance. When you were seven Elizabeth took Brandon from the house at Windswept Bay and disappeared. Your father wasn't able to locate him before he died."

Gage laughed gruffly. "Tell me? How hard is it to tell someone something like that?" Apparently harder than he thought considering his dad had died trying to figure out how to break the news. "I could have helped look for him."

Larry pulled his glasses off and rubbed the bridge of his nose. "Sit down, Gage. And I'll tell you what I know."

Anger boiled up inside him. It had been building since he'd found the first photo of his dad and his secret life. The life that he'd looked happier and more satisfied in than Gage had ever known him to look. The life where he'd had a kid who he'd carried on his shoulders. The son he'd sat in the sand and built sandcastles with…both things he'd never done with Gage.

"Why don't you do that?" He sat back down and stared at Larry. "Shoot. Give it to me straight."

"Shar, you've got to snap out of this."

Jillian looked up from where she was digging in one of the front flower beds of the resort. She had a full landscaping team to direct and delegate and yet she still had to get her knees and hands into the dirt at least once a day. Shar sat on a large landscape boulder and stared at her.

"I'm just sitting here. Is that a crime?"

Jillian let out an exasperated breath. "Sharleen Sinclair that's exactly the problem. You don't just sit. And for you that is a crime. Now, I do not lose my temper all that often, and surely not as much as you do. But you are about to put me over the moon if you don't snap out of this. You know good and well that you have been moping around for three weeks and I'm just not going to stand for it any longer. Either you get on a plane and fly to New York and fix this, this thing between you and Gage. Or, you get back to being my Superwoman sister who is invincible and determined and...you. That's you, Shar not this woman of hesitation."

They glared at each other.

Shar was being a jerk. Alex had told her the same thing. And yet she persisted in being hard to handle. The problem was, she wasn't sure about anything right now except that she missed Gage. All she'd been able to think about was how he'd told her he loved her and she'd told him basically that he didn't.

And now he was gone.

Jillian stood and put her hands on her hips and studied her. "But that's the problem isn't it? My sister who used to know exactly who she is suddenly isn't sure about that anymore."

Shar sucked in a breath and looked away.

"Honey." Jillian sank down on the rock beside her. "What scares you? We all change. Evolve. If you love the guy then it's okay."

"It's not exactly that. I mean for the longest time I

did think that. That if I gave into the emotions I felt when I was with him that I would lose myself. But, now, I just don't know how to admit it. I mean I know I love him and I want to tell him…but he left and he hasn't called. What if he changed his mind."

"You get up and you pack your bags and you get on a plane and you go tell him how you feel. It's that simple. Get it out in the open."

"What if I'm too late? What if I'm not too late and he finds out I'm irritable, and bossy and hard to get along with sometim—"

"He knows that already. Everyone does," Jillian said with a husky laugh. "Stop kidding yourself. You rescue everything—now get up and go rescue yourself."

Shar thought about that. And she stood. "I need to go home and think."

"Good. Don't worry about anything. I'll come by when I get off and pick up Rufus. He can stay with me."

"I didn't say I was going."

"You're going and you know it."

Shar rolled her eyes. "Okay, yes I'm going. But if he rejects me I may never speak to you again."

Jillian laughed. "Get out of here. Go. Or I'm going to start throwing dirt clods at you."

"Fine." Shar started for the parking lot and then turned back and grabbed Jillian in a hug. "Thanks, sis. And I'll speak to you no matter what happens."

Jillian hugged her back. "I know. Now, up, up and away. Go make your dreams come true."

Shar laughed and headed toward her car. This time she'd follow through and she wasn't coming back until she found him. Until she came clean and told him the truth.

*I love him.*

And it scared her to death.

She was tossing clothes into a suitcase when Rufus started going crazy barking in the living room. "Calm down, Rufus," she called. When he didn't stop and then she heard someone knocking on the door, Shar stopped yanking clothes out of her closet and went to see what was wrong. She stopped when she saw Gage on the deck, Rufus stood with both front paws on the window, and his little tail wagging ferociously as he barked his cute little head off.

Shar's pulse took flight right along with the jet-fueled butterflies winging their way around inside her chest.

"Open the door, Shar. Please," he called.

She finally reacted and moved to the door. "What are you doing here?"

"Seeing you." He reached down and picked up the wiggling ball of fur and laughed as he petted Rufus then he set the pup down and took a step toward her.

She wanted to throw herself into his arms but she held herself back by sheer willpower. "You've been gone for over three weeks. No phone call. No checkup on Mustang. On Rufus." *Or me.* "Just gone."

He smiled, slow and completely disarming. "You missed me."

"You just left."

"You missed me." He stepped further into the house and closed the door behind him. She took a step back and he took another one toward her. "Admit it."

She didn't say anything. *A girl had to have some*

*pride.*

He wrapped an arm around her and yanked her close. "I missed you."

"You have an odd way of showing it." *What am I doing?* She was going to run him off again.

He chuckled. "You told me I had things I needed to take care of. And so I did. Now I just have business here. And you're part of it. The most important part."

Shar couldn't breathe. She had dreamed of being in his arms again and now she was. She just wanted to melt into him and stay there. "Where have you been?" she asked softly.

"Finishing unfinished business, my father's will reading included. And now I'm here. And you can't tell me I'm confused or any of that other stuff you said that night. I love you and I'm here. And until you tell me there is nothing between us I'm going to stick around."

She stared at him and fought back the sting of tears. And then, she melted and threw her arms around his neck and pulled his head down and kissed him.

He smiled beneath her lips and then he joined in

the kiss.

After a long breathless moment she pulled back. "I've missed you so. And I was about to get on a plane and come find you."

"Oh yeah, now you're going to give me a big head. I can see the headlines: *Shar Sinclair comes after her man.* I like it a lot. "

She laughed. "Oh, is that what you are?"

"Exactly. And I'm giving you fair warning that, maybe not today or tomorrow, but when you're ready to get past thinking I'm going to hold you back from saving the world, I'm going to put a ring on your finger. But we're going to slow this down and I'm going to court you right. Like you deserve to be courted."

She smiled. "Courted?"

He nodded and kissed the tip of her nose. "We'll take it long and slow, dinner, movies, save some sea turtles along the way. And then when I think the courting has been long enough to make you believe my love is realistic and forever I'm going to get on my knee and ask you to marry me. But only after a year or maybe two."

"You're teasing."

"No. I'm actually serious. It's going to kill me but I'm going to do it. Because I can't live without you, Shar."

"I can't live without you."

His expression went completely serious. "You mean that?"

"With all my heart."

"Wow, that went completely too easy." And with that he bent his head and kissed her. Shar wilted in his arms as his warm breath mingled with hers.

When he finally broke the kiss, Shar wasn't sure her world would ever stop spinning. He took her hand, led her over to the couch and pulled her down into his arms.

"I honestly didn't expect you to welcome me back so easily. I hoped but I wasn't sure."

She cupped his face. "I came after you that day. I went to the airport, but you'd already gone. And then you never called."

"I wanted to. I picked the phone up a thousand times. But I didn't let myself make the call. I wanted to give you some time. And I did have unfinished business that had to be taken care of with the company and…" he paused. "Shar, I found out I have a brother."

Shar gasped. "You do? Where's he been?"

"I don't know. It's a long story and I'll tell you. But his mom took him and they disappeared. My dad's detective has just found information that makes him think he might be back in this area. I'm going to find him. It just might take some time."

"Does he know you're his brother?"

"We don't think he does. But I need to find him. For one, I want to know him. He's my brother. And also, he's now half owner of everything my dad had. He needs to know that."

Shar hugged Gage. "I love you, Gage. And I'll do everything I can to help you find him."

He kissed her again. "I knew you would. But that will come in time. Right now, I want to start that courting."

Shar smiled. "That sounds like a perfect idea."

And then he kissed her again. This time with such gentleness and emotion that Shar could feel his love in every beat of his heart…as her heart and his heart beat together as one.

Just like they were meant to beat.

Excerpt from

# WITH THIS KISS

Windswept Bay, Book Three

# CHAPTER ONE

S har Sinclair stared at her reflection in the mirror and the amazing, but simple, wedding dress that made her look more elegant than she'd ever felt in her life. She was marrying the man of her dreams. And that said a lot since she'd never actually thought she wanted to marry and share her life with anyone. And then Gage came along.

And suddenly she had her dream man and she was anxious to share her life with him.

She stared at herself in the mirror wearing her wedding dress and she tried to calm the turmoil trying to go a little haywire inside of her.

Why was she feeling this way? A tremor ran through her, like agitation as she breathed in slowly filling her lungs and holding it a few beats. *I'm just anxious.*

As if to contradict her thought, her stomach tightened into a thousand knots. Twisted, tight knots that threatened to squeeze the cheese crackers she'd eaten for lunch right out of her.

Nothing said non-elegant more than upchucking while wearing her wedding gown.

Shar exhaled heavily and shook herself.

*What is wrong with me?*

At the rate she was going she'd have an ulcer before her wedding was over.

"Is Gage here yet?" she asked.

Her older sister, Cali pushed a shiny strand of blonde hair behind her ear and smiled with assurance. "Not yet. But I'm sure he'll show up soon."

Shar moistened her dry lips. Instantly Jillian was

at her side with a tube of gloss. She and Jillian were two of a trio of triplets and though they didn't look alike they did share a keen sense about how the others were feeling which Jillian acknowledged in the look she gave her and her words, "Stop being a nervous wreck. And here, at the rate you're licking those lips they'll be chapped before Gage gets to kiss you in the ceremony."

Cali smiled into the mirror. "True, and that isn't the fun way to get them chapped."

Shar laughed despite her nerves and let Jillian run the rosy gloss over her lips. She was not used to having this much makeup on or her sisters hovering so much. But it was sweet and she was grateful right now to have them beside her.

"I've never worn so much makeup or lip gloss in all my life," she reminded them. "Gage may not recognize me when he finally gets here."

Jillian rolled her eyes. "He'll recognize you."

Tears suddenly pricked at her eyes. And a wave of panic rolled through her.

*Where are you Gage?* Three months ago she was

afraid of losing her independence and today she couldn't get his ring on her finger fast enough. If only her man would make it to the church on time they'd get this ceremony out of the way and start their lives together.

She looked at the clock…one hour to go and he was not here with his groomsmen getting into his tux. No matter what Jillian and Cali said, it wasn't right. He'd told her he couldn't wait to be her husband. That he'd be there ready and waiting to put a ring on her finger and to kiss her breathless. But he wasn't here. And she could deny it all she wanted but the truth was that her groom was missing.

"Relax, Shar. He'll be here." Cali gently rubbed Shar's back and their gazes met in the mirror once more. "He will be here," Cali enunciated each word carefully.

Always the encourager her older sister was trying hard to do just that.

"He said he would be here early. It's now inside of an hour and he's missing."

Cali's expression tensed. "He's not missing. He's

just running late or something."

Not a patient person, Shar gritted her teeth. Patience had never been her strong point, if she wanted something she went out and got it or acted. She was strong-willed that way and it worked for her. Waiting did not. "Jillian, please poke your head out the door again. Just to make sure he's not out there. Something isn't right. I feel it and there is no denying it."

Both her sisters stared at her and knew she'd reached her limit.

"It's just cold feet," Cali said, still trying one last time.

Jillian's brow knitted. "No, I can't imagine it being cold feet. Cali, you were on your extended honeymoon when Shar was moping around for weeks after Gage had left the island. She was climbing walls when she didn't think he was coming back. This is not cold feet."

Shar sent Jillian a grateful look for finally acknowledging that she wasn't overreacting. "Nope, no cold feet here. I love him. More than I ever dreamed was possible. I mean, because of my love for him I look at my life, that I was so protective of, and now am thrilled to get to share it with him. Not horde it away just for me." She felt weak-kneed suddenly and she couldn't breathe. "It's…where is he?" she gasped as tears surged up and threatened to overcome her. "I need to get this dress off and go find him." She grabbed for her zipper.

"Wait!" her sisters exclaimed together.

Jillian rushed forward and put her hands on Shar's. "Just wait, Shar. You can't take your dress off. People will be arriving soon. He will be here. He's still got over forty-five minutes."

Shar glared at her triplet. "You're right." She shook her head hoping to clear the panic from it. "This is so not like me."

Cali wrapped an arm around her waist and gave her a one armed hug. "Come on little sister. It's time for you to sit down. If Olivia were here she'd tell you to chill out."

Olivia. Once again her other triplet hadn't made it to one of their weddings. Shar had been worrying about her lately too. She wasn't calling much and though she said she was coming there was always an excuse at the last minute. Olivia had missed Cali's wedding and now hers.

"I wish Olivia had made it. I'm worried about her. This isn't like her either."

Cali handed her a glass of water. "Shar, you cannot fix everyone. Yes, you are Superwoman in my eyes with the way you rescue sea turtles and watch over the injured ones at the Sea Turtle Hospital. But, you worry too much for a straight shooter like you. Olivia is fine. When she's ready to come back home she will. Right now she's busy keeping the Hollywood elite out of hot water. She'll come home when she can. Until then we just need to let her live her life."

"True," Jillian agreed. "This is about you anyway and you're adding stress to your beautiful day that doesn't need to be here."

Shar's heart was thundering and her stomach had coiled into a thousand knots now. "You're right. I just wish he'd found Brandon. He'd hoped that in the two months since we set this wedding date that the private investigator would have good news about his missing brother. But the promising lead he thought he had hasn't come through."

"I can't imagine how Gage must feel. Just learning he has a brother at the reading of his father's will." Cali glanced at Jillian and Shar saw them struggling to be a unified front for her.

She rubbed her forehead. "I can understand him wanting to find Brandon and to have him at the wedding. We can't imagine having no family at all, we have such a huge one. But when you've just had your dad and then lost him...it's different. Surely..." her words trailed off as she left her thoughts unspoken...surely he hadn't decided not to show because his lost brother hadn't been found yet.

"Maybe something will turn up while you two are on your honeymoon." Cali encouraged once more.

"Yes, maybe it will." Jillian looked hopeful as she headed toward the door. "I'm going to go walk to the parking lot and see if any of the guys have heard anything."

"Thank you," Shar said in a rush, pushing away any thoughts about Gage not showing on purpose. He would be here. "And let me know the minute you know."

Jillian shot her that calming sweet smile of hers. "Well of course." She laughed gently. "Take deep breaths and relax. I'm on this."

That was just it, Shar needed to be on it. She was after all a control freak and she knew it. When the door closed behind her she heaved a heavy sigh. "And so we wait."

"Yes," Cali said sitting on the chair beside her. "And don't think I'm not watching you and know what's running through your head. Don't even think about going to the bathroom and climbing out the window to go hunt for him."

Shar laughed...because that was exactly the thought that had just crossed her mind and she'd been thinking she would do.

He shouldn't stop.

But he couldn't pass it up and so Gage found himself pulling into the boat docks just as a police car flew past him heading down the road with his siren blaring.

The moment Gage heard the siren he'd thought of the Sea Turtle Hospital's rescue ambulance, the one that usually meant Shar was near. But it had a distinctive siren that he could recognize instantly and so he'd known it wasn't the turtle ambulance.

As he parked his car and got out another police car raced down the road past the entrance of the boating dock. He paused to watch it turn down a side road. Something was going on and he wondered if Levi, Shar's brother and chief of police, would be involved. He hoped not because the wedding was happening within the hour and Shar would want Levi and all of her brothers at the wedding. She'd want him there more, so why was he stopping here?

He pulled his phone out and looked at the address on the text message he'd just received. He hoped Shar wasn't having a nervous breakdown or about to come looking for him. He should be there and he would make it on time.

He just needed to see if his brother was on this

boat.

He expected his phone to ring any minute and he hated that he was running late. But, he'd gotten the email and then the address texted to him from the private investigator only moments ago. He'd been heading to the Windswept Bay Resort where the wedding would be held but the news he'd been waiting for had finally come.

His brother was indeed living in Windswept Bay.

They'd been searching for Brandon Jackson the message said that his name was now BJ McCall. That he'd been adopted by his stepfather around a year after his mother had disappeared with him.

The message said that he was supposed to be on his boat at this dock.

Gage was thirty-one and his brother was about four years younger than him and had been missing since he was about three, so today would be ending about a twenty-four year long search.

What would Brandon think about having a brother?

Gage looked at his watch again. He had an hour to

get to the resort so he could marry the woman of his dreams so he better get this show on the road.

He stepped onto the dock and headed down the planked runway between the rows and rows of sailboats and deep sea fishing boats. It was a quiet day. Seagulls drifted overhead like lazy kites dipping and soaring and watching for fish in the water. Many of the boat slips were empty as with most gorgeous days fishing was a priority of the bay area. Or just heading out to enjoy the blue waters of Windswept Bay. He stopped when he reached the Morning Glory, the name of the boat listed in the email and the text.

It was a nice sized deep sea fishing boat, but from the fact that it was nearly five o'clock in the afternoon and most of the charter boats were out with paying clients and this one was sitting in its slip made him wonder why. The sound of the mutterings coming from the cabin had him pausing before he stepped onto the deck. With little time to spare he boarded the boat.

He had a wedding to get to.

Standing Shar up was not an option.

It would hurt her too deeply "Anyone on board?"

he called.

There was no answer. But Gage had heard the mutterings so he knew someone was inside the cabin. "I just want to ask you a couple of questions," he called louder. There was no way he was walking away before possibly meeting his brother.

He heard murmurs of what sounded like two voices. He waited and then a man with lighter hair than Gage's came up out of the hull. He had a little grease on his hands and he was looking down as he wiped them on a rag. Gage tried to find a resemblance to himself in the chiseled, tanned skin and the squared jaw. But there wasn't any.

"What questions?" the man asked as he lifted his gaze and pinned Gage with icy, teal-blue eyes.

Gage's adrenaline kicked up as he looked into the exact same eyes as his. And also the same eyes as his father's, Milton Lancaster, eyes. It was an undeniable genetic gift that he'd evidently passed down to both of his sons.

The impact that he was staring at his brother was almost overwhelming.

It felt as if the boat was hit by a tidal wave as the reality set in and the world rocked around Gage.

"What can I do for you?" Brandon—or BJ asked, briskly, his gaze taking in Gage's tux then shifting back toward the opening to the cabin. "I'm thinking you're not dressed for an outing today. And I hate to break it to you, buddy, but if you just got married your new bride is not going to want to go out on a fishing charter at this moment."

"Actually, I'm on my way to get married." Gage thought of Shar. "And you might be wrong about that her not wanting to be on the water at least." He held out his hand. "I'm Gage Lancaster by the way."

Gage watched the other man's expression for any signs of recognition. He saw none. Nothing, not even a flicker of anything that hinted that Brandon knew who he was. But Gage *knew* this was his brother. If there had been any doubts about it not being Brandon the eyes proved it to Gage one hundred percent.

His brother stared hard at Gage's outstretched hand and then he looked down at his grease streaked hands. "I don't think your bride will appreciate you getting grease on your wedding fingers. Maybe you should leave and come back after the honeymoon." He hitched a brow and his eyes narrowed. Then he yanked his head toward the dock. "It's a good time to leave."

So his brother wasn't the most sociable guy. One of the first business rules Gage had learned from his dad, when he was not much older than ten was to never take no for an answer. "I actually came to ask a few questions."

His brother's jaw tensed and his gaze shifted toward the cabin. Gage followed the movement and thought he saw a shadow flicker in the opening. Something didn't feel right.

Was there someone standing just inside the cabin doorway? "Is there a problem?"

BJ's blue eyes chilled. "*No.* Look, I need to get back to work on my motor." His eyes had narrowed as they shifted once again back to the cabin. "And you look like you need to get to a wedding."

Gage should leave. He should turn around and walk off that boat and get the dickens to the resort and marry Shar. But this was his brother and something did not feel right.

And Gage had always had good instincts. So instead of heading off the boat he took a step toward the cabin. "I'm running late, but I've got time. I need to ask you a few questions."

BJ took a step toward the cabin to block his path. "You don't want to ask me any questions. Go on. Get off my boat," he snapped.

"Too late," a man growled and stepped from where he'd been hidden just inside the cabin. He held a gun in one hand and he pointed it straight at Gage. "If the man wants to ask questions he can do it while you're driving this boat down the coast."

Gage's stomach clenched and he thought of Shar standing alone waiting for him.

What had he done?

# More Books by Debra Clopton

**Turner Creek Ranch Series**
Treasure Me, Cowboy (Book 1)
Rescue Me, Cowboy (Book 2)
Complete Me, Cowboy (Book 3)
Sweet Talk Me, Cowboy (Book 4)

**New Horizon Ranch Series**
Her Texas Cowboy (Book 1)
Rafe (Book 2)
Chase (Book 3)
Ty (Book 4)
Dalton (Book 5)
Treb (Book 6)
Maddie's Secret Baby (Book 7)
Austin (Book 8)

**Cowboys of Ransom Creek**
Her Cowboy Hero (Book 1)
Bride for Hire (Book 2)
Cooper (Book 3)
Shane (Book 4)
Vance (Book 5)
Drake (Book 6)
Brice (Book 7)

# About the Author

Bestselling author Debra Clopton has sold over 2.5 million books. Her book OPERATION: MARRIED BY CHRISTMAS has been optioned for an ABC Family Movie. Debra is known for her contemporary, western romances, Texas cowboys and feisty heroines. Sweet romance and humor are always intertwined to make readers smile. A sixth generation Texan she lives with her husband on a ranch deep in the heart of Texas. She loves being contacted by readers.

Visit Debra's website at www.debraclopton.com

Sign up for Debra's newsletter at
www.debraclopton.com/contest/

Check out her Facebook at
www.facebook.com/debra.clopton.5

Follow her on Twitter at @debraclopton

Contact her at debraclopton@ymail.com

If you enjoyed reading *Somewhere With You* I would appreciate it if you would help others enjoy this book, too.

**Recommend it.** Please help other readers find this book by recommending it to friends, reader's groups and discussion boards.

**Review it.** Please tell other readers why you liked this book by reviewing it on the retail site you purchased it from or Goodreads. If you do write a review, please send an email to debraclopton@ymail.com so I can thank you with a personal email. Or visit me at: www.debraclopton.com.

Made in the USA
Coppell, TX
24 July 2021

59432004R10116